Last Night Had Turned To Ice,

creating a fairyland, irreplaceable and priceless.

Susan and Stix walked the ravine, where pine branches were weighted with snow, and sunlight created prisms and rainbows. Susan couldn't turn without seeing a spectrum of emeralds, sapphires, rubies. Ferns hugged the forest floor, all coated with more crystal lace.

"See why I couldn't wait to wake you up?" Stix murmured.

"Yes." Both the illusion and the reality had a terrible fragility, and perhaps adding to the specialness was knowing that the fairy-tale world wouldn't last. The sun was out. The world was wet and dripping. In a matter of hours, Stix's woods would just be woods again, not a lace-and-prism land for princesses.

Susan suddenly felt as fragile as the view. Nothing in nature was permanent. Even as nature created things of incomparable beauty, she set them up to change, not endure. Flowers wilted. Ice melted. And people who believed themselves indestructibly, powerfully, immutably in love found themselves mistaken.

Dear Reader:

I hope you've been enjoying 1989, our "Year of the Man" at Silhouette Desire. Every one of the twelve authors who are contributing a *Man of the Month* has created a very special someone for your reading pleasure. Each man is unique, and each author's style and characterization give you a different insight into her man's story.

From January to December, 1989 will be a twelve-month extravaganza spotlighting one book each month with special cover treatment as a tribute to the Silhouette Desire hero—our *Man of the Month*!

Created by your favorite authors, these men are utterly irresistible. Love, betrayal, greed and revenge are all part of Lucy Gordon's dramatic *Vengeance Is Mine*, featuring Luke Harmon as Mr. May, and I think you'll find Annette Broadrick's Quinn McNamara... *Irresistible*! Coming in June.

Don't let these men get away!

Yours,

Isabel Swift
Senior Editor & Editorial Coordinator

JENNIFER GREENE

DANCING IN THE DARK

SILHOUETTE *Desire*

Published by Silhouette Books New York

America's Publisher of Contemporary Romance

SILHOUETTE BOOKS
300 East 42nd St., New York, N.Y. 10017

ISBN: 0-373-05498-X

First Silhouette Books printing May 1989

Printed in the U.S.A.

Books by Jennifer Greene

Silhouette Desire

Body and Soul #263
Foolish Pleasure #293
Madam's Room #326
Dear Reader #350
Minx #366
Lady Be Good #385
Love Potion #421
The Castle Keep #439
Lady of the Island #463
Night of the Hunter #481
Dancing in the Dark #498

Silhouette Intimate Moments

Secrets #221

JENNIFER GREENE

lives on a centennial farm near Lake Michigan with her husband and two children. Before writing full-time, she worked as a personnel manager, counselor and teacher. Mid-1988 marked the publication of her twenty-fifth romance. She claims the critical ingredient to success is a compassionate, kind, patient, understanding husband—who can cook.

Her writing has won national awards from the Romance Writers of America, *Romantic Times*, and *Affaire De Coeur*. She has also written under the pen name Jeanne Grant.

One

___

"Now I don't want you to think I'm setting anything up."

"Sure, Kay."

"This has nothing to do with matchmaking. I just want you to meet a *friend*."

"Sure, Kay."

"And if you don't take that patient expression off your face, I'm going to knock your block off."

Stix's grin was as lazy and slow as a spring-morning sunrise. "What's all the complaining? I'm here, aren't I?"

"Only because I bullied the life out of you," Kay said dryly.

Stix shrugged off his sheepskin jacket and shot a wry look at his chair. The University of Idaho's lecture halls—at least *this* one—were old, stately, and had seats built for midgets. Kay fitted fine, and in fact had room for a colored garble of scarves, gloves, hat, purse and coat.

He dropped his six-foot-six frame down next to her and immediately had a problem with his knees—primarily, where to put them for the next two hours. An evening lecture on biological anthropology was an ordeal of torture he would only have suffered for Kay.

"You think I should call home?"

He couldn't help grinning again. "You've only been away from Mitch and the twins for twenty minutes. I think they're probably still alive and well."

"I just know he's feeding them suckers," she said glumly. "I had such big hopes that Mitch would make a great father—gentle and loving, but with good control. What a joke! The girls blink their eyes at him, and the discipline's all over. They're probably tearing up the house with their trikes."

"Probably. Want to go home and see?" Stix asked.

Kay slid him an admonishing glare. "One more word and I warn you, you'll be in big trouble."

"What did I say now?"

"It wasn't what you said, it was the way you said it. Resign yourself. We're staying, and if you'll just give her a chance, I know you're going to like Susan. She's a terrific person, and her lectures are fascinating. You think the kids would pack in here like this if she were boring? And a little higher education isn't going to hurt you."

Stix, watching the last of the crowd find seats as the lights dimmed, figured he could nap. In preparation, he scrunched his shoulders in the metal-armed chair, yawned, and half-closed his eyes.

"No napping," Kay whispered.

There was a problem with old friends. They either knew you too well, or not at all. Stix had loved Kay for as long as he could remember—loved her enough that her talk of the twins and her husband produced an old, nagging, weary ache; loved her enough that she had never—and would never—guess his private feelings for her.

He also loved her enough to suffer through her incessant attempts at matchmaking. Without exerting any monumental energy, such as raising his eyes, he watched Kay's newest marriage prospect cross the lecture-hall stage to the podium.

To his surprise, she wasn't bad. Kay's last choice had been doll height. He guessed Susan to be a respectable five-foot-seven, and she definitely had legs—nice, long, sexy legs, accentuated by a sweater dress in a shocking red. She slid onto a stool behind the podium and switched on its small light as she addressed the group. "Ready to get started?"

Her voice had a hoarse, husky texture, like whiskey on the rocks. Most men's bedroom-fantasy women had voices like that. Stix figured she had a cold.

As silence, and the lights, fell, he languidly studied her features from the fifteen-row distance. She had a curly pile of ash-blond hair, styled short, free-for-all and windblown. She was currently using a pair of tortoiseshell glasses as a hair band. Her mouth was a small but distinctive slash of red. Her face was oval with elegant, classical lines that were spoiled thoroughly by a tipped nose. Few blondes had dark eyes. She did— huge, dark eyes that examined the audience in a comfortable, familiar fashion.

From what Kay had told him, Stix had expected a solitary nervous introvert—a lady who'd taken up celibacy since a love affair had gone bad, a lady who was holed up in her lonesome shell and desperately needed a friend.

Kay, much as he loved her, could hand out more bull than a used-car salesman. The lithe, slim woman perched on the lecture stool radiated confidence and energy. Maybe she wasn't a traditional beauty, but she had a sparkle and vibrance that was always going to catch a man's attention. And her smile—all subtle tease and promise—was the frosting on the cake.

"As usual, I can promise you this is not a lecture you'll ever hear from your mother." When her audience chuckled, she groped for the glasses on her head and propped them on the tip of her nose. Her grin faded. She cocked her head toward the audience in an expression of no-nonsense business.

"Falling in love," she announced, "is one of the fanciest, sneakiest tricks Nature ever pulled on mankind."

Stix found himself rubbing his jaw. Granted, his knowledge of biological anthropology was zilch, but he'd assumed her talk would be an intellectual dissertation on old bones and long-dead civilizations.

"Nature packed our bodies with all kinds of clever chemicals. We have adrenaline that lies dormant until we need it—for times of danger and stress. And we all have another chemical in our bodies called phenylethylamine, and this particular chemical is as powerful and addictive as heroin." She paused.

"Falling in love is usually considered a subject for poets, not scientists. In fact, many of you may consider the phrase to be a romantic cliché. You would be mistaken—dangerously mistaken—if you believe that. The mush is not only real, but a condition totally unique to the human species. We *do* fall in love. We *do* hear bells ring and feel our hearts go pitterpat, and those dreadful symptoms have a factual, biological base—a direct surge of phenylethylamine in the brain. We're talking the power of a chemical that makes nuclear energy look pale. *Never* misjudge the power of nature."

Next to him, Kay murmured, "Didn't I tell you she was good?"

Stix failed to answer. Once she really got going, Susan shoved the glasses back on her head. She pushed up her sleeves, then absentmindedly pushed them down again. She slid off the stool and started pacing, dragging the mike cord with her. At first he mistook her constant motion for nervousness, but that wasn't true. Her face was as mobile and expressive as her body, and her body simply had too much energy to sit still. The kids responded to her talk with periods of silence broken frequently with murmured chuckles and laughter. They obviously knew her and what to expect. Stix didn't.

She claimed that nature used this chemical—this phenylethylamine business—to coax mankind into propagating the species. As with other common drugs, though, the human body eventually developed a tolerance to it. The heady symptoms of falling in love didn't—and were never intended to—last. Once the chemical's reaction faded, in real-life terms, the couple either got divorced or settled into a relationship of comfortable boredom.

"And that's part of nature's plan, too, of course. Our contemporary society gets all upset about the current high divorce statistics, when we forget that the monogamous relationship was never natural to man. Nature has never given a hoot about morals. Nature's interest is survival, and the key to survival for any species is in reproduction. If you think about it, monogamous relationships are the worst possible thing that could happen to our long-term genetic pool."

Stix wasn't sure at what point he was actually charmed. She was so damned sassy, that was part of it. She stood or sat or swung those long legs around the ministage, and gently, teasingly reduced the sacred institutions of love, marriage and children to biochemical terms.

Humor, not cynicism, dominated her huskily delivered message. She claimed that in real life it was tough to fight nature's city hall. It was a mistake, though, to fall under "phenylethylamine's spell" without looking at the broader picture. Nature's plan never included happily ever afters. That was tough duckies, but that was life.

Stix found himself increasingly captivated—not by the lecture but by the lady. Susan had an infectious laugh, a way of tossing back her head, a way of stopping the crowd dead with a smile. She delivered her material with merciless honesty—"these are the facts; we *will* face them"—that made him wonder if she was that hard on herself in real life. And there was pride. Every time he saw those long, long legs swing around the podium, he saw pride and confidence. He couldn't imagine why an image of vulnerability kept dawdling through his mind.

At a quarter to nine, she abruptly stopped talking and glanced at her watch. "What is this? Why didn't somebody yell out that I was talking right through your break? Go on, get out of here, all of you—we'll finish this up next Wednesday night."

A collective sigh rippled through the lecture hall, and then noise picked up. Notebooks slammed closed. Books dropped. Coats got zipped and buttoned over the building buzz of conversation. Next to him, Kay slapped a knit hat on her head and shot him a self-satisfied smile. *See* it said. I told you she was something. "Now I talked her into having coffee with us after the lecture, and that wasn't easy," she scolded him. "You be nice. No looking bored. No yawning."

"I've been up since 5:00 a.m.," he reminded her.

"I don't care if you've been up since dawn. Straighten up, for heaven's sake." She reached up and adjusted the collar on his sheepskin jacket. Her gesture was protective and maternal, the only emotions he'd ever aroused in Kay. "You're such a mess," she said despairingly. "I've always known a good woman could make something of you, but we're talking such an uphill project. You know how long you've had that jacket?"

"Fifteen years," he guessed.

"I'll make Mitch take you shopping."

"Your husband likes me," Stix reminded her. "He also rates shopping up there with water torture, just like I do. And Kay?"

"Hmm?" She was reaching back for all the paraphernalia she inevitably took with her. Stix camped with less equipment than her purse held.

"What I'm wearing's irrelevant, isn't it? You made pretty clear we weren't talking about a *date* here. You just wanted someone to meet Susan because she's lonesome and shy, a real recluse. From what I was given to understand, the poor thing's been all cooped up, never gets out; she's real nervous around people—"

"I don't remember going *that* far," Kay interrupted.

"Trust me. You went further."

"She *is* shy."

"I can see that."

Wielding a briefcase, gloves and a long wool coat, Susan was weaving up the aisle toward them. Her progress was slow because she had to stop every few feet to talk to her students. Once and then again, Stix heard her throaty peel of infectious laughter.

"Real shy," he said deadpan.

"That's not the real Susan."

Stix didn't know who the "real" Susan was, but shortly thereafter a distinctly real woman exuberantly threw her arms around Kay. For several minutes, neither woman would have heard a fire alarm. They both talked nonstop and wasted no time breathing. Who'd lost weight, who'd gained weight, how were the twins, she liked her dress, she liked her hair, how was Mitch, the Halloween sale at the mall...as far as Stix could tell, the two women friends hadn't seen each other in at least two weeks. Mercy.

Susan peeked at him twice—he tried hard to wipe the unholy grin off his face—but he had no idea what wheels were clicking in her head until she suddenly stopped talking. Abruptly, her eyes widened. Her very pert lower lip sagged. Her hand flew to her heart. "*You're* Stix?"

"Guilty."

"Good Lord." He was finally close enough to see that her eyes were cocoa brown and as full of sassy sparkle as the rest of her. Her gaze whisked first to Kay and then back to him. Slowly, slowly back to him.

Like a fastidious butcher evaluating hung beef, she swung a full circle around him. His fanny got the first look, as if a woman had priorities, but from there she examined in ascending order. Her gaze started with his moccasins, then inched up his long lanky legs—he didn't *believe* how blatantly long she stared at the bulge in his jeans—then moved on up to chest and shoulders.

"Umm..." Kay's face was changing color, something like a nervous streetlight.

Susan didn't dawdle at his throat and chin, but lingered on his mouth like a cat waiting for cream—heaved a huge passionate sigh—and finally, lovingly, surveyed his disheveled brown hair. By that time, she had a palm arched over her brow as if trying to see the top of a mountain on a sunny day. "He's *everything* you said, Kay. Everything. He's absolutely adorable! A little lean, but overall—*what a man*."

Kay's uneasy smile expressed concern that her friend had lost all her marbles. Susan was oblivious. For the first time, her eyes met his—*damn*, she was a devil!—and her tone lowered to a sultry whisper. "Are you good in bed, sweetie?"

Stix had always moved slowly by choice, not because he wasn't quick. Grave as a judge, he drawled, "You wouldn't believe how good."

"I knew it! No infectious or social diseases?"

"Not a one."

"Already we have something in common! Isn't this exciting? How many children do you want, Stix?"

He was starting to have a good time. "Twelve."

She made a moue. "I'd only wanted ten. Could we—dare we—should we—risk finding out if we're capable of a compromise?"

"Eleven?"

"He's *wonderful*," Susan crowed to Kay.

Kay cleared her throat. "Why do I have a feeling," she said dryly, "that I'm being drawn into a sucker play? Is there anything *wrong* with wanting your two favorite people to meet each other?"

"Am I complaining?" Susan's eyebrows winged in offended surprise. "Stix, are you complaining?"

Stix looked as helpless as a six-foot-six man can, but that was a little like hoping a house could shrink to the size of a pillbox. "I'm being good as gold. In fact, I promised Kay I would be as good as gold. She gave me the rules. I'm supposed to be *nice*. No falling asleep. No yawnin'—"

"Come on, you two." Kay grabbed them by the arm and propelled them toward the door. "And to think I volunteered for this outing. Both of you *try* and behave over coffee, would you?"

Kay was the only one who'd brought a car—neither Stix nor Susan had bothered, since most distances in the university town of Moscow were walkable. The October night was crisp, black and peaceful. Main Street closed up by nine, but the softly lit restaurant was still open. Kay did a general's job of herding her less-than-disciplined troupe of two to a booth at the back. Stix obediently allowed himself to be maneuvered between the two women and closest to Susan.

Most diners had finished eating, but a dessert tray was being passed. Once the women ordered coffee, Stix latched on to a napoleon, a slice of cheesecake and a fat wedge of chocolate brownie. Not for the first time since the drive over there, Kay rolled her eyes toward the ceiling. "He doesn't always eat like this," she assured Susan.

Susan murmured, "Do you always eat like this?"

"Always," Stix admitted. "I also kill for cherry doughnuts."

"Ah, well. We'd probably all kill for something. I've always loved a man with an itsy-bitsy violent streak...."

Over the past twenty minutes, Kay's voice had increased in volume, as if her companions were deaf. "Stix, did I mention that Susan likes to explore caves just like you do? Spelunking, isn't that what you call it?"

"You're kidding?" He shook his head in wonder. "Yet *another* thing in common, Suze."

"Should we rush right home to bed or get the marriage license first?" The same sprite who'd competently lectured to over a hundred college students less than an hour before now batted eyelashes up at him adoringly. "You're so gorgeous. Can I feel your biceps?"

Kay cupped her chin in her hands. "You're both going to get tired of this soon," she said weakly.

"Honey, you can feel anything—*anything*—you want." Stix finished the brownie and dusted off the crumbs. "When instant chemistry's this powerful, inhibitions have no place. This body is yours. Don't limit yourself to biceps."

"I certainly don't want to." Susan stirred sugar in her coffee, her voice as bland as fake cream. "I'll tell you, Stix, it's a heavy temptation to throw you on the table and take you right here and now."

Stix aimed for the napoleon. "The table won't give us much room. Don't you think the carpet would give us more space?"

"Oh, sweetheart, let's not have our first quibble over such a silly detail when my heart's pounding like a freight train."

Kay made one last attempt to look severe. "If—and I'm not saying I will—I'm just saying *if* I promise never to matchmake again as long as I live, would you two consider having a nice normal conversation like real people?''

Stix shot a perplexed glance at Susan. "I thought this was what she wanted."

"I thought this was what she wanted, too. Can I try a bite of that cheesecake?''

"Sure. Kay, do you want some?''

"I want to go home to my husband and children—people who love me."

"We love you," Stix assured her.

"Tremendously," Susan agreed, then turned to Stix, "You think she's learned her lesson?''

"*Yes,*" Kay sang out.

"I don't know." Susan took a long sip of coffee. "This is the third time in six months she's tried to set me up. I don't know what bullying tactics she pulled on you, Stix, but I gave in from sheer exhaustion."

"I'm sorry. *Very* sorry. Very, very, *very* sorry."

"She sounds suitably chastened," Stix mentioned—a total lie. Kay was seconds away from dissolving into chuckles, and then they were all laughing.

They closed the restaurant at midnight, and the three walked Kay to her car, still erupting in occasional chuckles. All laughter died when the wink of Kay's taillights disappeared as she turned in the distance, although Stix wasn't sure why.

No other cars were on Main Street this late. The night was windless, the moon bright. Susan stood next to him, hands slung in her pockets and her shoulders hunched in her gray wool coat. Her smile hadn't dimmed, but he could see it was going to. The game and the laughter and the teasing had been for Kay, not for a stranger she didn't know from Adam.

"I wouldn't seriously make fun of her for the world, you know. I love Kay; she's been a good friend for years."

"And for me." Stix tried to remember the last time he'd felt awkward around a woman, and couldn't. The past few hours had sped by so fast. They'd handed each other lines like an experienced comedy team, like people who'd known each other for a dozen years. From the moment Susan had so gravely devoured his body with her eyes, he'd recognized a spirit of mischief and humor that rivaled his own.

Now, rather suddenly, it occurred to him that he didn't know her at all. And that he wanted to.

She wasn't like Kay. Although comparisons were unfair, Stix knew he had been guilty of making them before. Kay had been his first date, his first love and, God help him, the only woman he'd ever been capable of loving. He'd never chosen that pit; he'd never wanted it, but wishing never stopped a river. For some men, there was only one woman.

Usually that old, painful bullet hit him early on when he met a new woman. If there was no crossing his river, he never failed to protect the woman he was with. Over the years he'd become a master at developing natural, comfortable, no-stress relationships. Nothing was different tonight.

Except Susan. He couldn't seem to stop looking at her, not because of any fancy sexual vibrations; she was just so...human. Her hair looked like crushed gold under the streetlight, and over the hours her makeup had worn off. He saw the faint peppering of freckles across her nose, the vulnerable shadows beneath her eyes, her pale skin. She'd been "on" all evening. Not now. The competent, vital lecturer had worn down. The incorrigibly teasing friend had grown weary. Life was a zesty tang, but even a kittenish life-lover needed rest sometime.

He wanted to touch her cheek. If it were any other woman, he would have given in to the impulse and offered a giant bear hug as well. Life was tough. Affection was free. And no one had ever misunderstood Stix's natural expressions of warmth before, but he had a feeling Susan might.

That instinct had no rational base. Everything she'd said and done all evening had led him to believe she was a quick, confident, secure lady who knew exactly who she was and what she wanted. He decided that his reaction was just from the streetlight, the silence, the night. The image that she was fragile—easily hurt—refused to leave him.

So he kept his hands at his sides. "Which way's home?" he asked lightly.

"Up A Street. And not far, just up a few blocks."

"I'm off of B on Third. You cold?"

"Not at all."

But she was. Her shoulders were still hunched, her cheeks beginning to glow color. When they started walking, he automatically adjusted to her pace, which earned him a smile. "You're always stuck slowing down when you're walking with someone, aren't you?"

"What can I say? I was built to keep up a competitive lope with a giraffe or a horse."

"Pity. Not too many of those around Moscow."

He chuckled, relieved that her sparkle was back and the image of vulnerability gone. Where the steady stream of conversation had seemed natural in the restaurant, now silence rested easily between them. He knew why. In spite of the laughter, in spite of the game with Kay, Susan had made it dominantly clear that she wasn't in the market for a mate. So had he. The stress and tension that inevitably cluttered a first meeting between a single man and woman was unnecessary. That suited him. And it obviously suited her.

For four blocks, dry leaves rustled above their heads in a sudden, restless breeze. If there was a sizzle in the air, Stix marked it off as the sniff of autumn. Winter would bring a lalapalooza of a wind in Idaho; but not now, not yet, not this night. More than once, he found himself shooting a grin down at her. Just as easily, she shot back her own feminine smile.

The easy companionship lasted until they reached the cross of A and Third. When he automatically stepped off the curb in her direction, she stopped him. "Don't be silly. You don't have to walk me home. I walk these streets all the time at night. It's perfectly safe. And Kay said you own the restaurant—the breakfast place on Walker, isn't it? So you must have to be up at dawn."

"You're not that many blocks out of my way," he insisted.

Again she shook her head. "Maybe not, but it *is* out of your way, and why bother? I'm twenty-nine, far too old for coddling, and you need your beauty sleep, shorty. Go for it." At his hesitation, she distracted him with the sudden warm curl of her lips. "But I did have a good time. Thanks. I haven't laughed like I have tonight in a really long time. It was a good evening."

"Yes."

"Kay, much as I love her, was never going to hurt from a tiny lesson in letting adults be adults. I think it's the twins. She's had this impulse to mother the entire human race ever since they were born."

He chuckled, then recognized her fast patter for the diversion it was. In those few seconds, she'd taken three steps away, then four. She whisked out a "G'night, Stix. See you again sometime?" Then she turned and kept walking.

He had no excuse to chase after her. As she said, the streets were safe. The walking-home-after-a-date courtesy didn't apply because this hadn't been a date. Still, he found himself staring at her retreating back, feeling oddly uneasy and unsettled.

She was obviously fine. Her step was springy, her head tilted high. There was just something about her. He didn't want to think about her walking the streets alone. He wanted to know she was locked in a warm house somewhere, safe, secure, protected. He watched her walk in light, then shadow, and he couldn't shake the illusion of a special, painful, vulnerable fragility.

He stuffed his hands into his pockets and straightened, aware he was tired and not thinking well. The illusion was clearly nonsense. Susan Markham was a woman who could obviously take care of herself, and did.

Stix never intruded where he wasn't wanted, and never had a problem erasing a woman from his mind. Ever. No exceptions.

He turned away, and with a brisk step, headed for home.

Two

The fresh autumn morning was irresistible. A soft mist cuddled in the valleys and a sunrise was streaking the hills. The old maples and oaks glinted with dew-drenched colors—tobacco and amber and russet—and the sidewalks were a leaf-shuffler's dream.

Within minutes, Susan was huffing and puffing.

She loved Moscow. Three years before, she'd thought she'd have a hard time transplanting from Indianapolis to a small town, but that hadn't been true. Moscow had all the cultural advantages of two major universities within twenty miles of each other. A few hours' drive in any direction and there were riches: south, Hell's Canyon and the wild Snake River country; west, Spokane and shopping to please the most hardened sale addict; Coeur d'Alene was just north, and to the northeast were the lure and lore of mountains—a spelunker's paradise of abandoned silver mines and caves and ghost towns. Moscow itself was a charmer.

But the darn town was built on hills. The few miles' downhill walk coming home from classes was a breeze. But getting there was slightly tricky without mountain-climbing gear. Think of the inches you're toning off those thighs, Susan consoled herself.

But the thought wouldn't take root. As it had the night before, her mind abandoned its usually rational thought processes. On the one hand, she was reasonably pleased with how she'd handled Stix. He couldn't have known that she'd reacted to that first meeting as if two emotional bullets had been jammed into her chest by a sniper.

However, Stix was solely responsible for her fitful night's sleep. And a half hour later, as she faced a lecture hall of sleepy-faced students, she discovered that Stix was also responsible for her having forgotten her notes, pen and glasses.

True, she had a minuscule tendency toward absent-mindedness before she'd met the man—most days she considered it lucky if she remembered her purse. However, she normally *never* forgot the things that were important. Lessons in life, for instance.

Three classes, a rushed sandwich and staff meeting later, she climbed to her third-story cubbyhole of an office. Tossing briefcase, a sheaf of files and purse on her desk, she shed her coat and slipped off her high heels.

Relaxing took a time-honored set of rituals. The sleeves of her dark blue sweater had to be pushed up, then the day's mail and memos sorted through while she brewed herself a cup of tea from the university's forbidden-hot-pot-that-everyone-had. She found a mug, but then couldn't find a spoon. The bottom desk drawer had to be pulled out to make a perch for her stocking feet and her earrings tugged off.

The rituals done, she settled the stack of anthropology tests on her lap, ready to work. She fully intended to work—the very instant the man she'd met the night before stopped sneaking into her consciousness and destroying her concentration.

Everyone in town knew Stix. Susan had known his name long before Kay had mentioned it. He owned a breakfast place—the kind that was open before dawn and closed before noon, the kind where the lonesome popped in for their first cup of coffee of the day and came back every morning—not for the food, but for the company.

Kids, old biddies, the police, the lovelorn... everyone liked Stix. You could trust him. You could talk to him. He never broke a promise and he never told a secret. Females of all ages claimed that a daily hug and grin came free with the coffee, and everyone knew he brewed the best this side of the Rockies.

More relevant, by reputation he'd dated every single woman within a two-hundred-mile radius. Women didn't usually sing praises about a rover and a roamer who spread his affections around that thin. Stix was the exception. The word was liberally spread that he was one of the last decent, safe, no-pressure good-time, lovably uncomplicated single men left in America.

Unfortunately for Susan, the man was just plain poison.

"Hi."

Without looking up, she returned an automatically cheerful "Hi." She didn't have to look up to know who was standing there. Not that superstitions dominated her life, but Murphy could have been her first cousin. When you had no time for the flu, that was when you caught it. Think too long of the devil and the devil inevitably appeared.

Stix ducked for the low archway, then poke-slow ambled in. "Got a free ten minutes?" Since he was already setting a long flat box on her desk and dragging off his jacket, her response appeared token. Rather than look at him, she peeked into the box. The dozen cherry doughnuts were still warm and reeked—*reeked*—of calories.

"And to think Kay calls you a friend. How could you do this to me?"

He tossed his jacket on a stack of books in the corner, took two doughnuts from the box and dropped, legs sprawled easily, into the spare wooden chair opposite her desk. "They say never drink alone."

"There's no brandy in these."

"I don't have a problem with brandy. I have a problem with doughnuts. They're just no good alone."

"Heavens. I never realized."

His grin was quick, potent and incorrigibly boyish. For long seconds, his gaze lingered on her face. Her toes curled, for no real reason, and then his attention was diverted to her desk and windows and double-stacked, cluttered bookshelves. Her office had just enough turnaround space for a woman who kept her knees together. A man Stix's size could barely exhale without bumping into something.

Watching him, Susan took a bite of doughnut and prayed it would settle the sudden uneasy jump in her stomach. Prayer didn't help, and neither did the doughnut. The symptoms of damp palms, zipping heartbeat and a flush of tension and heat could have been caused by several things. With any luck, she was getting a cold. At twenty-nine, though, she knew damn well when she was attracted to a man.

It would have helped if Stix were drop-dead handsome. Most noticeably good-looking men came packaged with vanity and ego—easy turnoffs for her. Stix wasn't such a looker. He just had something that, annoyingly, made her go all warm inside. Maybe it was the boyish shag of dark hair over his brow, maybe the rugged stretch of shoulders, maybe the way his old jeans defined a man's hips, a man's hard thighs. His face was windburned. His fisherman's sweater was a thousand years old. His boots had the creases and shine of old leather; and such big feet!

Such a sinfully natural grin. And he had a basset hound's innocent eyes that said, Love me, how can't you help it? That was part of the problem. He looked warm-bloodedly huggable. He looked like a man that a woman should take home, feed, tuck in and wrap up on a cold winter's night. He looked, to Susan, like a man who would make a long, slow, lazy, natural, unforgettable lover.

Since she had never had a long, slow, lazy, natural, unforgettable lover, she couldn't imagine why the thought crossed her mind. She certainly didn't want it there, and the first doughnut settled like a chunk of lye in her stomach. Defying all logic and pride, she reached for another.

"The books look forbiddingly impressive," he commented.

"Thank heavens. I accumulate them for the effect. I've had big hopes for some time that somebody will take me for a fancy intellectual."

He foraged through the white box again. "You're getting behind," he warned her. "I'm on my third. You can't very well keep up all your fancy intellectual strength on a mere two doughnuts."

She sighed and finished off her second. "I had big hopes of staying a size nine this year. I don't know why I don't just glue these on my thighs and have done with it. That's where they're going to end up anyway, and it's all your fault."

"I suppose I could have brought carrot sticks."

"Bite your tongue, shorty."

He chuckled. "You've got miles to go before you ever reach plump. What's all this worry?"

"Who's worried? So I do ten hours of aerobics tonight. Good grief, you're polishing them off at the speed of sound. You indulge this vice on a daily basis?"

"My mother used to claim I came out of the womb eating her out of house and home."

"I can believe that." Susan started to reach for a third doughnut and then abruptly remembered she was a woman of strong will and self-control. Some days, anyway. To keep her hands out of trouble, she wrapped them firmly around her tea mug. "I'm going to do you a big favor and not ask if you ever played basketball. But it *would* be nice to know if you had a real name besides Stix. Or is that a deep dark secret?"

"The birth certificate read Stanley Nicholas Sperling the Third, and no, that's no big secret. As long as you understand that any mention of that name outside this office will mean the last doughnuts you'll ever get from me."

"The Third, hmm?"

"Do you have a death wish? Behave, Suze," he warned her.

She kept telling herself that he didn't know her well enough to tease her. And she didn't know him well enough to feel so natural with him. Telling herself things didn't help. His right boot eventually found a home on top of her desk. She eventually made him a mug of coffee. He eventually depleted the doughnut supply, and she kept laughing.

Exploring caves was a mutual hobby. They both traded spelunking tales, but that was their last claim to a serious conversation. He'd broken an arm when he was six. She'd broken a wrist when she was thirteen. As a kid, he was a marbles champion and a failure at chemistry. As a kid, she was a frog collector and a failure at home ec. He was in a wedding once where he'd lost the ring. At her senior prom, she'd fallen in the mud.

Heaven knew where the silly subjects kept coming from, but a few minutes stretched into an hour. Then, as unexpectedly as he'd shown up, he stood, stretched the kinks out of his knees and reached for his jacket. "Done with your classes for the day?"

She nodded. "Thursday, my classes are over with by noon."

"So..." Once his jacket was on, he jammed his hands into his back pockets. "Do you have the time to continue this crazy conversation over dinner?"

"You can't be hungry!" She motioned to the empty doughnut box.

"That was just an appetizer. Besides, it'll take a little time to put some serious food together. Notice I didn't ask if you were willing to cook? I didn't forget that failure in home ec."

"Wise," she murmured dryly, and finally found the good sense to remind herself of the same. Let's practice a little wisdom, Susan. She was too perceptive not to notice the subtle change of expression in his gentle, dark eyes. His crooked smile was suddenly less than sure. His hands were still. The casual invitation had no hidden pressures or catches, but the offer hadn't been lightly made. He'd enjoyed the time with her.

She'd enjoyed the time with him, even more than last night. Life was full of humor, but not shared laughter. Susan was comfortable with most men, but most men didn't make her feel heady and happy, spring-fever wistful and . . . wanting.

Never mind how harmless, Susan was smart enough to avoid black cats. "Thanks for the offer, but I have to turn it down," she said regretfully. "I'm stuck with four hours of test grading to do tonight, I'm afraid."

His smile never wavered, but something died in his eyes. He responded so quickly that she knew he'd taken her trumped-up excuse for what it was. "No problem. Maybe we can work out something another time."

"Sure."

Only she wasn't off the hook quite yet. He cocked a leg forward and made a token effort at a dead-serious frown. "So I'm leaving, as soon as I get my hug for bringing the doughnuts."

She could handle nonsense. "Hey. Did I ask you to destroy my diet for this entire week?"

"No hug?" He looked as crestfallen as a kid who'd just struck out on a little-league team.

"No hug," she said severely.

"You're a hard woman, Suze."

She wished, so hard, that she were. When he had gone, she found herself sitting as immobile as a statue

and stuck with a smile that hadn't yet faded. Stuck with
the aroma of doughnuts and this winsome, sexy curl in
her stomach and the fierce, irrational wish that she'd
hugged him.

But the darn man loved Kay.

Before moving here, Susan had a stereotype of small
towns as being cruel—gossip oriented, critical, judg-
mental. Not Moscow. There was no hint that anything
inappropriate or intimate had ever happened between
Kay and Stix, because it hadn't. But the whole town
knew he loved Kay and always had. Nothing had been
directly said, and Susan had gradually understood that
nothing would be. Stix was well loved, well liked, well
respected. If he had a weakness, he'd never allowed it
to hurt anyone, affect anyone, trouble anyone. The
town protected him with silence and showed respect for
a good man by ignoring the whole affair.

In fact, there was no "affair" to ignore, except that
the so-gentle hints she had picked up before had been
slam clear last night. She saw the way he looked at
Kay—like a big, growly, affectionate bear...waiting to
be kicked in the teeth.

You couldn't help whom you loved. She knew that
well. You could love someone from here to forever, but
there were no guarantees that that "someone" would
return the emotion. Maybe it was so easy to recognize
those life-lesson scars in Stix because she had a few of
her own.

As a child, she'd been kicked from foster home to
foster home, hoping just once that it would catch. As a
girl, she'd approached every date with the pocketful of
hope that there might be someone she could matter to.
And as a woman, she'd run into Karn. He'd been a man

who wanted to love her and a man who had tried, embarrassingly hard.

Karn's problem had been the ghost of a past love, and her problem had been survival when the affair was over. Too many people had *tried* to love her in a lifetime. Apparently the job was tougher than digging ditches. Three years ago she'd had the self-esteem of a dead turkey and the self-worth of a wilted daffodil. It was the lowest period in her life.

And she was never going back to it. Discovering self-respect and self-reliance had been a long haul, but the keys to survival were well learned now. It wasn't that she no longer yearned to be loved; but facing the possibility of love, and Susan, just didn't go together. A smart woman didn't put herself in situations where she got kicked in the teeth, and a smart woman recognized trouble when she saw it.

Stix was a warm, funny, gentle man. His lazy grin made her toes curl and his eyes made her hormones sing bluesy torch songs. She liked him, but that was as far as it was going to go. He wasn't over an old love, and she'd played second fiddle to ghosts before. She'd ended up in shambles, and she'd rather eat knives than repeat the experience.

Nine days later was the first Saturday in November, and the University of Idaho's homecoming football game. The two o'clock starting time coincided with a bone-chilling sleet. The bag of popcorn in Stix's hand was starting to freeze, and icy rain slithered down his neck even before he reached the bleachers.

Neither the weather nor the team's rare losing streak bothered the crowd; the stands were packed and the mood was rowdy. He automatically headed to the top—

he wasn't likely to block anyone's view if he sat in the higher seats—and he climbed at his usual lackadaisical pace because there was no point in hurrying just to find a wet seat. A collective roar shuddered through the stadium—kickoff time—and when he looked toward the playing field, he spotted Susan instead.

She was sitting high, around the home-team thirty-yard line. He was climbing high, around the competitor's thirty-yard line. Barring a nonexistent helicopter, getting anywhere near her would take a monumental amount of energy. Wasting energy was never on Stix's list of priorities, and he reminded himself that her "No" signals had been crystal clear on both occasions they'd met.

She was sitting alone, though, give or take the surrounding masses. A family was on one side of her, a clutch of boys on the other. Even from the distance, he could see her red-cold nose. A thick wool scarf was snaked around her neck a dozen times—as scarlet as a beacon and covering her mouth. But the crazy woman wore no hat; the sleet turned wet gold the instant it hit her hair.

She suddenly stood up, mittened hands flying to her hips in response to a football play. His gaze stayed glued to her instead of the field—not that he wanted it to. He'd offered her a little no-strings company. She'd turned him down. He guessed that she'd been hurt and simply didn't want to play, not even at casual friendships. He respected that choice. He always respected a woman's choices.

His size-thirteen boots started turning, though, and headed down instead of up. His downward momentum was perfectly logical. It had nothing to do with respect, but with hats. If he was going to spend another nine days worrying about her for no known reason on this earth, he didn't want to worry about her home in bed with the flu.

Susan, intent on the game, had no idea she had company until a stocking hat was flopped over her eyes and a bag of popcorn appeared in her lap. She twisted her head to the seat behind her, and abruptly found her shoulders wedged between two bony knees.

Her heart recognized Stix with a thump and a kick. For an instant, all the screams and raucous noise faded to a whoosh of silence. Packed bodies and faces blurred. Only Stix was in focus—the ruddy color in his cheeks, the damp shock of hair on his forehead, the incorrigibly slow grin.

"I kept looking." He motioned vaguely to the stands. "Couldn't find anybody else in the whole stadium who might be willing to put up with my knees behind them."

"How many did you have to ask?"

"Hundreds. You're not going to send me away, too, are you?"

I should, she thought. She'd worked the memory of that incorrigible grin out of her mind. She'd faked herself into believing the attraction was exaggerated. She didn't want to laugh with him again, didn't want any more exposure to trouble...but then his knees cuddled her shoulders when he leaned forward.

"Where's your hat?"

"Forgot it." The way he looked at her could make a woman forget a lot of things, but that, Susan knew, was because he had the gift. Every female in town from seven to seventy was under the impression that Stix found them special. To avoid being taken in by those lethally warm brown eyes, she glanced down, found his popcorn bag in her lap and peered in. "Your popcorn is soggy, but I understand. You were probably terrified that you couldn't make it more than two hours without food of some kind."

"Anybody ever tell you that you have a long sassy streak?" The crowd diverted him with a unisoned groan for an interception.

"The game just started and already they're killing us," she said glumly.

Amusement danced in his eyes. "Suze. We normally have one of the best teams in the conference, but not this year. We've lost seven games out of seven. What did you expect?"

Not to see you here. "I had big hopes of seeing the big ox with the seven on his jersey show some smarts on the football field. He sure isn't trying in my eight o'clock anthro class."

"You can't flunk the team quarterback!"

"I'm not flunking him. I'm just going to pin his ears to the wall with a tutor. The boy almost had me fooled into believing he had a serious future as a jock. Are you watching him play?"

Stix, momentarily, seemed to be watching her. He reached down and pushed a strand of hair from her cheek.

Either the contact unsettled her, or the bemused intensity in his eyes did. She faced front for the next half hour, which was perfectly reasonable since twisting back like a pretzel was physically uncomfortable. On the field below, play followed play. From the sky above, sleet kept knifing down.

She missed the plays, forgot the sleet. Stix hunched over her like a tent. His knees locked her in the private V of his body, and when his arm wasn't sneaking down for a handful of popcorn, he used her shoulders for armrests.

To construe any of that contact as intimate or sexual was ridiculous. Pounds of wet jackets, scarves and denim separated them. All he was doing was keeping her warm, offering some nominal body protection against the cold gray sleet. And his conversation was no more than a running commentary on the game. Sort of. A mildly roared "Block that kick!" was accompanied by an admonishing "Snuggle back, silly. You wanna freeze?" and then a "Kill that turkey!"

She already knew that he took casual contact for granted. There was no justifying the blood rushing to her head, the heat zinging through her veins, the cluster of erotic awareness in the private parts of her body. Possibly she had low blood sugar. Possibly she was going out of her mind. Possibly her hormones were sick and tired of celibacy.

Possibly she was more inexplicably, dangerously, physically aware of Stix than any man in years. But that seemed highly unlikely.

The crowd suddenly stormed to its feet. She bounced up, too, trying to see what was happening. Over the deafening cheer of "Touchdown!" the stands went into a jostling, backslapping, hugging frenzy. She dashed a smile up at Stix—her way of celebrating the hard-won six points.

Stix had other ways of celebrating. Exuberantly he snatched her. The popcorn bag went flying. Laughing hard, he lifted her high and close. Faster than she could blink, his mouth smacked down on hers. The bear hug—even the kiss—wasn't anything different from what a hundred other people were sharing.

Only for her, that "highly unlikely" nonsense abruptly became dominantly, potently real. Somebody pushed a mute button on the crowd, and a whoosh of silence roared in her ears again. She felt only Stix.

His lips were cold, resolute, mobile and utterly silent. Crushed against him, her nostrils flared for the scent of wet wool, old leather, and man. She promised herself that she didn't have to be drawn under. She already knew desire could sprout up faster than dandelions in spring grass. This is nothing, she kept telling herself. But it was. Dammit, it was.

His first kiss was an exuberant slam of pressure, but it was over in seconds. She tore her mouth free, but wasn't quick enough. She caught the whip-stung look in his eyes, the shock of surprise, his sudden stillness. And then his arms inexorably tightened around her and his mouth searched for hers a second time.

If she hadn't been dependent on him for balance, she could have pulled free. Maybe. His lips skimmed hers, then lightened, skimmed...and then fused. He took her mouth as if he'd just found forbidden treasure. He tasted so lonesome, so lost. She heard him murmur her name. He made it sound like hunger.

A shudder shook him and she saw the raw look in his eyes, the ice rain streaming down his wet skin. He seemed unaware. He kissed with wonder. He kissed with tenderness. He kissed as if he needed her—*her*—and her arms wrapped around him because they had to.

He didn't seem to understand what he was giving away. This wasn't a view for other people. As if her instinct was to shield him, she let her mouth be molded under his, warm and yielding, yet helpless and angry. Big strong men weren't supposed to be this vulnerable, but those wild kisses kept coming. Some cradled, some crushed. He was appeased for a long moment when his tongue found hers.

But then she wasn't. Hot syrup never burned like this. Need, simmered on a long-forgotten pot, exploded. Texture, color, focus shimmered on one man, one emotion. Desire had flavored her life before, but she had always done the wooing, the wanting, the needing. No one had ever responded to her like this. No man, ever, had seemed to need her like this.

She had the sense to recognize something she was afraid of, something she couldn't handle. Stix simply complicated that good sense. He kept drawing her down and under, where the water was dark and deep. His eyes, his mouth, his arms, banished fantasies about being cherished, about being loved, about there being one man she could matter to. Such illusions were dangerous and foolish, but for those brief moments, her delinquent heart soared toward the promise like a fistful of suddenly released balloons.

His mouth finally lifted from hers. She heard the drag of his breath even over the shrill screams of the crowd. Tension, as hot and special as summer lightning, passed between them. Then their eyes met.

She saw his confused, disoriented gaze, the wedge of his frown, the tightened muscle in his cheek. A raw, thick lump filled her throat and she erased every reckless fantasy she'd ever had.

Slowly, he lowered her to her feet. He bent down and picked up her fallen hat. Big, awkward hands pushed her hair up under it again. Shock victims had more color and he was missing his lazy grin. His thumb brushed her cheek. "You all right?" he asked softly.

"Yes." But she wasn't. The stroke of his thumb on her cheek was as tender as an apology, as subtle as guilt.

She'd seen it all before. Too many times. Karn may have been the last straw, but even before him, she'd picked up outstanding skills at reading a man's body language. For that raw instant Stix had stared at her as if he had no idea who she was.

He hadn't known who she was, because he hadn't wanted to. He'd been mentally kissing someone else, not her. Even before she met him, she'd known he loved someone else.

What a fool she was. And even more of a fool to feel so... wounded.

"Susan?"

She forced a smile to her lips. Fool's pride. It must not have been good enough, because his knuckles curled under her chin and she was stuck facing those fathomless dark eyes of his again. "I don't know about you," he murmured, "but I feel just like someone pulled the rug out from underneath me."

Three

———

Fun, wasn't it?'' Susan asked cheerfully.

"Fun?" In his time, Stix had kissed his share of women. He was extremely fond of the pastime, but no woman, including Kay, had ever shattered his sense of reality or buckled his knees before. His pulse was still frisky, his throat felt full of rust. To add insult to injury—and with all the lack of conscience of a hit-and-run driver—Susan blithely whisked her head toward the football field. ''They made the extra point. Did you see?''

''No!''

''Heavens, we're blocking everyone's view. We'd better sit down.''

He might have bought her casual dismissal if he hadn't really looked at her. Her face was drained of color, her mouth less than steady, and—too carefully—she avoided eye contact. ''You're right,'' he

DANCING IN THE DARK 41

agreed, and without another word grasped her wrist, ignored the scrunched bodies all around them, and pulled her up.

"Are you crazy?"

Finding a path through the crowd was like threading a needle. He headed upward, with Susan's wrist gently manacled just behind him, until they reached a block of empty seats in the top row.

"Did we trample half the stadium for a reason?" she murmured wryly.

"Quit trying so hard to be *light*. You're as shook-up as I am." He hunched down next to her, aware his tone was irritable. He wasn't happy. The whole world knew he could nap through an earthquake, and here he was, completely confused.

"Stix, everything is fine," she said gently.

But nothing was fine. His hands were sweaty. His heart was drumming. Some man had just come on to Susan in the middle of a football stadium with all the finesse and delicacy of a blowtorch, but it couldn't have been him. And the same woman who had shattered his legendary solid nerves was now patting his knee, maternal fashion.

"We bogged down for a little chemistry, didn't we?" Her whisper was light, whimsical. "Why not? Kisses are fun. Nature set it up that way. Both of us knew there was nothing more to it, didn't we?"

He didn't know what he knew or didn't know, except that his professor—the one working so hard to reassure him—had hair like a wet mop. Damned if the woman could keep a hat on. And maybe she wasn't looking at him, but she chattered faster than a wren at reveille the minute he touched her.

"Relax, Stix. There's no problem. You, especially, are used to this kind of thing."

He stopped pushing her hair under his hat. "Used to what kind of thing?"

"Come on, you know what I mean. From what I hear, half the women in town get their day started with a kiss and hug from you. You're obviously an affectionate man. Heavens, I'm not criticizing! I think it's terrific that you can take casual contact for granted."

He blinked. Hard. Nobody but a woman could deliver censure in a compliment. Sure, he hugged a few women in the course of most days, but hell—Mrs. McCarthy was eighty-three and carried a cane; Julie Kneberg might be only sixteen but she'd just lost her brother. And there were others, but that was just affection. *Honest* affection. Susan made it sound like he slung out hugs like cheap dog food.

"And then there's Kay."

The icy wind smacked his exposed skin when he turned. "Kay? What does *Kay* have to do with anything?"

"I'm sorry. I never meant to bring up a touchy subject."

"Why on earth would *Kay* be a touchy subject?"

As if she were experienced at soothing big, wounded bears, she slipped her hand in his and squeezed. "I don't want to make you uncomfortable—"

"You're not." She was.

"Good. Because I'd like to believe friends can be honest with each other." She freed her hand and became terribly busy putting on her mittens. She'd seen the look in his eyes when Kay's name was mentioned. She didn't need to see it again. "You've loved her for a long time."

"If for some reason we're still talking about *Kay*, you may have noticed she has two small children and a happy marriage. I stood up at her wedding. In fact, I'm godfather to her two devils, and Mitch and I play poker most Wednesday nights. So I don't know what you're thinking or what you're trying to say."

"Just that emotions don't shut off as easily as faucets. Just that we can't will ourselves to love or unlove people because we want to. Just that...I think I can understand if you need a friend to talk to." She let that settle, then softly, swiftly continued. "All I started out to say was that you seemed upset about that kiss, like you thought you needed to make apologies. You don't. This is just me, Susan, the last person on earth who would ever misinterpret a little chance chemistry. These things happen. What's the harm? We're both adults... and I'll be darned! We just stole the ball away from them!"

She flashed him a wholesome smile.

He flashed her one back, swallowing the sensation that he'd just been caught with his fly open in a crowd. His feelings for Kay had long been a source of guilt and dissonance, but one source of comfort was the sure knowledge that no one knew how he felt. Susan's perception hit like a strap below the belt. He felt exposed, distracted, and defensive—until he stole another look at her.

Her attention was enthusiastically riveted on the ten-yard line.

The football was being passed at the fiftieth.

His frown deepened and his eyes softened. So...Suze was not so calm, not so casual. He hadn't imagined her sweet, wild, explosive responsiveness. He hadn't imagined her coming alive in his arms, all yearning hunger,

all passionate longing. She was apparently still shocked
by the disturbing potency of that embrace and she just
didn't want him to know. He realized with an instinc-
tive flash that thumbscrews and a rack wouldn't get her
to admit what had happened.

Her nose was red and her bangs were wet, and the tilt
of her shoulders was rigid with pride. He'd missed that
before, just as he'd missed the face-slapped sting in her
eyes before.

*I swear I don't know how I hurt you, Susan Mark-
ham.* It took him a moment to reach that conclusion,
the same moment in which he reviewed the contents of
her fast, pretty speech. She thought he took women
lightly. She thought he was using her. She thought he
was hung up on another woman. He felt the slam of
guilt—an old friend, particularly since Kay uncon-
sciously sneaked into many an encounter—but in this
case, that slam wasn't fair. No man, not in this life,
could kiss Susan and think of anyone else but Susan.

"Stix? You awake up there?"

"Sure." He couldn't seem to stop looking at her. All
that brash, sassy confidence. All the right words to dis-
tract and rattle a man. Her calm, clear brown eyes . . .
*You're such a faker, Suze. You're as scared as I am. And
how the hell could you have any doubts about how
special you are?*

She waved her hand in front of his face. "Are you up
there? There's an interception on the field. You're supposed to yell and swear. It's a rule."

Before the game was over, she gravely explained the
rules by teaching him every swearword appropriate to
football, fed him hot dogs from the wandering vendor,
and coaxed him into talking about the trials and tribu-
lations of the restaurant business.

Later, after the game was won, she melded into the diffusing crowd with excuses of something she had to do. Then, too late, he understood that she'd been taking care of him, Susan style. A four-year-old with a skinned knee not only needed a Band-Aid but also a kiss. When a grown man wandered into disturbing territory, he needed soothing, diverting, someone to tease and listen and appease. So she'd done that.

Stix was touched. But definitely not soothed, diverted or appeased.

Susan tugged the sweater over her head and gave her image in the bathroom mirror a wry look. There must be some reason she kept wearing red when she knew the color made her skin look washed-out. Insanity? Stubbornness? A latent rebellious streak?

She tucked in the sweater and sucked in to snap up her jeans. "Worry less about red and more about the cherry doughnuts, Susan Markham," she murmured, then glanced at her watch and flew.

It was six-thirty. She was due at Kay and Mitch's at seven, and before that had to come up with a purse, car keys, shoes and a jacket. She found the jacket in the suspended peach wicker chair in the living room. One shoe was hidden behind a froth of curtains, the other— who would have guessed?—was stashed neatly in her bedroom closet. Her purse was in plain sight on the peach Formica counter in the kitchen.

That left keys to find.

Her apartment—bedroom, living room and kitchen—took up the entire second floor of an old Victorian house that specialized in stuccoed walls, arched doorways, and a deplorable number of hideaway nooks and crannies. The first-floor owners, Nance and Dave,

couldn't afford the old white elephant without an upstairs tenant. From the first they'd been more friends
than landlords, which was a good thing. Some landlords might have balked at Susan's concept of decorat-
ing.

She loved peach with a passion. Anything that could
be painted, recovered or hung was peach, but the color
was broken by the clutter of books, plants, a collection
of crystal unicorns, eclectic paintings and unfolded
clothes. She frequently yelled at herself about the dis-
graceful mess, but not too loudly. This was her home,
her castle, her refuge. She'd never had any of those
three before, and as she indulged in peach, she indulged in her need to have her own things around her
where she could see them—not necessarily find them,
but see them.

"I'm going to use the spare set of keys if you don't
turn up soon," she warned the empty air. Then she
froze as she saw the time on the chime clock and
promptly followed through with her threat.

Five inches of fresh snow slowed down the drive. By
the Saturday after Thanksgiving, snow was to be
expected, and her Rabbit was good on slippery roads—
just not fast.

Stix had offered to pick her up, but it hadn't seemed
wise. Picking up reeked of "date." As it was, over the
past three weeks Stix had been trying to develop the
distinctly bad habit of trying to live at her place. He
brought doughnuts. He brought éclairs. He brought the
Sunday papers and once, a wrench to fix her leaky fau-
cet.

She'd approached every impromptu visit with full-
scale defenses on red alert, but ultimately it was tough
to be wary of a man bearing gifts of a wrench nature.

He hadn't touched her. He hadn't tried. She'd even ended up telling him foster-home tales—something she never did because she didn't want people feeling sorry for her. But Stix could relate so well. She knew he had a house, though he didn't seem to live in it. From the number and length of his visits, one could definitely get the impression that the huge man was homeless. How could she not take him in?

How could she possibly have been roped in to this humorous fiasco with him tonight? Stix had *claimed* he'd been roped in to baby-sitting Kay's twins.

"You trying to tell me Kay and Mitch couldn't find a baby-sitter in an entire town of college kids?" she'd asked him.

"Kay keeps finding them, Mitch keeps firing them," Stix had said glumly. "Come on, Suze. Save my rear end, would you? Lord knows I love them, but you must have met Kay's kids. They're miniature dragons. I can't handle this alone. Where's your mercy? Where's your compassion? Didn't you take some sacred vows as a Girl Scout sometime?"

She'd never been a Girl Scout, but that was neither here nor there. Every time Stix said "Suze," she had a problem. She hated the nickname, had always hated the nickname. When he said it, her blood heated to toast and her heart launched a love song. One could ignore hormones, she'd been doing it for a long time, but she couldn't ignore the issue of Stix and Kay.

She'd tried, as gently and tactfully as she knew how, to get him to talk about his feelings for Kay. She didn't want to pry. She wanted to help. At some point between the éclairs and the wrench, she'd grown to seriously care about this homeless waif of a giant. The only way she really knew how to help him was by defusing situations where he had to be around Kay.

A friend helped a friend. That wasn't complex. She had carefully and meticulously made it absolutely positive that she treated Stix as an uncomplicated friend. Men were too good at picking up unconscious sexual messages. She shook that unconscious good when it surfaced.

She'd had to shake it a lot lately. Stix was a gentle man. Unselfish. Generously giving. A man with his own rare style, his own implicit sexuality. A rare breed of loner and lover.

If his heart weren't already taken... She always ruthlessly stopped herself on *that* thought. Stix was not heart free. At any mention of Kay the man clammed up, and Susan had no intention of stepping off the sunny side of the street into quicksand.

After another twenty minutes, she turned into the niche of woods that marked the Cochran property. Kay's husband, Mitch, did more than okay for himself, but the regality of the stone-and-glass minimansion was destroyed by the set of carrot-nosed snowmen in the front yard. She was smiling as she reached the door.

Mitch formed a welcoming committee of one. "Come on in, Susie. I'll take your jacket. Kay's just finishing getting dressed, and Stix is already in the kitchen. You two are lifesavers."

"Believe me, the treat's on this side. I hardly ever get a chance to even see your kids." As he led her through the scarlet and cream living room, she vaguely remembered being nervous around Mitch when she first met him.

Built as solid as steel, he had a striking streak of white in his dark hair and a daunting set of life-etched lines around his eyes and brow. He'd seemed awfully austere and terribly serious, but that image had vanished the first time she'd seen him with Kay. When Mitch Cochran looked at his wife, his personal earth moved, and it showed. He didn't even try to hide it.

From that time on, whether or not he needed an honorary kid sister, Susan had stolen the role. Now she motioned to his gray suit and starched white shirt. "I hate to swell your head, but you're almost looking handsome. Where are you taking her?"

"Kay has her heart set on lobster." He scratched his chin with a grin. "I'd settle for an hour in the garage in the back seat of the car where no small voices could possibly interrupt us."

"Ah."

"She needs out of the house and a little space away from our angels. A little too much champagne wouldn't hurt her, either. But in the meantime..."

In the meantime, three steps down and they were in the kitchen. Backdropped by spotless pecan-colored counters and green plants that blocked every light source, two four-year-old girls stood in footed pajamas, holding hands. Nobody could take them for anything but a set. Both had freshly brushed, curly brown hair, clean faces with turned-up noses, angelic brown eyes and subdued, painfully shy smiles.

"Hi, Susie."

"Hi, Susie."

"Hi, sweeties." She dropped a kiss on both their foreheads and then straightened for a glimpse of her fellow baby-sitter.

Like her, Stix had dressed for romp-and-stomp children's play: tan cords and an old shirt open at the throat. He'd stashed his shoes somewhere. He'd also nicked his cheek shaving, which seemed to be a dreadful habit of his. Next to Mitch's dauntingly distinguished looks, Stix was a hopelessly sad-eyed giant bear.

The Lord only knew why her pulse suddenly stammered and missed. It wasn't fair. She had the increasingly terrible feeling that her heartbeat could pick out Stix in a cast of thousands.

Chemistry was controllable, but there was a look of strain around Stix's eyes that showed the pull of less manageable emotions. She'd seen the tension building over the past three weeks. Smudges of tiredness circled his eyes. His unholy grin was there, but tonight it was more pushed than easy. Darn it, she wondered. Was it that hard for him to be around Kay?

Susan automatically moved next to him and pushed up the sleeves of her red angora sweater, just as if she were preparing to do something hard and sweaty, like lay cement or panel a room; or show the big bear that she was one tough cookie when it came to friend protecting. Talk, however, had to wait.

"They're going to be good, aren't you, loves?" Mitch prodded his offspring.

"Yes, Daddy."

"Kay rented a Disney film, so you two wouldn't have to worry about entertaining them. That'll be done in about an hour, then a glass of milk and bed. Right, Kathy? Right, Kim?"

"Yes, Daddy."

"Hmm." Mitch sighed and motioned to the wine bottle on the curl of the counter. Susan's brows lifted at the Henri Bourgeois label. "That's for the two of you, after they go to bed."

"Mitch, are you crazy? That's hardly necessary," she chided.

Mitch was looking at his offspring. "Oh, yes, it is. In fact you're probably going to wish I'd left you hard liquor—even though they're going to be *very* good. Aren't you, girls?"

"Yes, Daddy." Angels should look so innocent, so subdued, so perfect. The one, Kathy, looked slightly hurt at the implications in her father's voice.

"Are we going to give Stix and Susie any trouble?" Mitch said severely.

"No, Daddy."

Kay swirled into the room in a swish of apricot silk, scent, and opals. Confusion inevitably followed. Kay, being Kay, never stopped talking. While Mitch did his best to thread his wife's arms into her coat, she had nine hundred sets of instructions, some sneaky teasing about the two baby-sitters spending time together, four kisses to deliver to her little ones, news to catch up on. And to Mitch she ended with, "You're *sure* we should go? I'm almost sure Kim had a slight sniffle this afternoon—"

"We're leaving." Mitch's hand patted his wife's bottom unerringly toward the door.

"Did I leave the number for the doctor?"

"You left them our entire phone book and enough first-aid supplies for a bomb squad," Mitch said patiently.

"Stix, did I tell you there was some leftover chicken, and Susan—Mitch, you're rushing me. I haven't even had five minutes to talk to Susan and I haven't seen her all wee—"

Mitch winked at both of them and closed the door while Kay was still midsentence. That was the first moment Susan realized she'd moved thigh-to-thigh close to Stix—protectively close, as if she were a lead shield against his exposure to radioactivity.

Kay, much as Susan loved her friend, was radioactivity in motion. Dressed up, she was past beautiful and her warmth and humor made her more so. The exact same qualities that made Kay a good friend made it all too easy to see why Stix had fallen in love with her. It had to be impossibly tough on him, seeing Kay so happy with Mitch.

When she tilted her head, she realized again how close he was. She'd carefully avoided physical contact but this was different. He was tense again—so unlike Stix—and there was a dark, dark look in his eyes that tore at her. She found a sprig of lint on his shoulder, the excuse to stroke, to comfort. *No one can understand more than I can. You really can't help who you love. Only you've got to see that she's happy, Stix. You have to get over her.*

"Susan." His grip closed on her wrist. Tension suddenly shimmered between them like a ripple in a still pond. Abruptly, the instant she severed the physical contact between them, it was gone. He ducked his head and drove a hand into his pocket. He came up with a nickel and flipped it. "Heads or tails?"

"What's the bet?" She had to be a crazy woman. There had been no tension. If there was going to be tension, it would have shown up in the past three weeks.

"How long are you going to guess we'll be stuck with the angels?" He covered the coin on the back of his wrist.

"Tails. And my guess is Kay'll never make it past nine before she starts worrying about the kids."

"I'll go for two in the morning." His eyes danced. "Don't underestimate Mitch in a romantic mood."

"She looked beautiful," Susan murmured.

"Kay always does."

Especially when compared to a woman who lost things, wore red and shouldn't and was beginning to feel hopelessly, dangerously drawn to a pair of melt-brown eyes. But she reined in that last thought before it galloped into an illusion. Love and Susan had never been more than that. "Hey," she said suddenly.

"Hey what?"

"Where are the angels?"

Their eyes met—both sets filled with alarm. The whole house was pin-drop silent. Like a runner who'd just heard the gun signal at the start of a track meet, Susan surged toward the kitchen door, which led to the living room. Instantly two screaming banshees scuttled to the tops of the couches with high-pitched laser guns. Wadded-up paper bombs soared through the air. A lamp tilted, threatening to topple. An ottoman overturned.

Stix, to be heard, had to bend by her ear. "You didn't seriously buy the shy, innocent routine, did you?"

"No, but I didn't exactly expect this!"

"This" was chaos. Total, instant, irretrievable chaos. Kay's house, so neat and orderly, was destroyed in minutes. Divide-and-conquer didn't work. Nobody wanted to read books. Nobody wanted to watch Walt Disney. They wanted a vicious war between the land of Tarmagon and the Evel Knievels of Ballgor. Following that, they wanted to play in the snow in the dark. Then some fool—Stix—stupidly suggested they make cocoa.

By the time three eggs were cleaned up—they broke when Kim was reaching for the milk—the kitchen looked like a marshmallow-and-chocolate fallout zone. Brushing-teeth rituals destroyed the bathroom. Then came silence. Total silence.

"We have to find them," Susan told Stix darkly. "It's not that big a house. How many places can they hide?"

"At bedtime? I'll bet they can hide out for quite a while."

"What do you mean, 'bedtime'? It's nine-thirty. It's an hour *past* bedtime. And we have to get this house cleaned up before Kay and Mitch get home. For heaven's sake, we're two intelligent, mature grownups. How did it all get away from us so fast?"

"Suze?"

She leaned up from where she'd been kid searching in the bottom of a closet. Stix's eyes had a pure-devil gleam. "You're having a wonderful time," he commented.

"I can't be."

"You are."

"I'm sure you're mistaken—" Her eyes popped open wide. "I just saw a speeding bullet fly past. Quick!"

Twenty minutes later, the two girls were carried upside down to their bedroom—a land mine of canopied beds, stuffed animals, miniature kitchen furniture and dollhouses. Susan wrestled one to bed, Stix the other.

"We're not tired," Kathy complained.

"Not at *all*," agreed her sidekick.

"So we'll have a story. You two like Uncle Remus?" Susan suggested.

Stix shook his head at her. "They like gore," he whispered.

"They're only four years old!"

"Do you want them to go to sleep or don't you?"

They were asleep three minutes after the monster story, but then it took a full hour of frenetic energy to restore any potential livability to the house.

Stix had just sprawled on the overstuffed scarlet couch when Susan padded in from the kitchen and threw herself at the opposite end. He straightened far enough up to get a good look at her over his knees.

Her socks were gone—wet from playing outside—and her jeans hems were still damp. Her red sweater was no longer tucked in and it had a cocoa smudge on the cuff. One sleeve was pushed up, one down. Her lipstick was gone. Her makeup was gone. Her bangs looked like toothpick sprigs, and the rest of her mop looked combed by the devil.

"Don't you dare saying anything, shorty. You don't exactly look ready to attend church yourself." The one eye she found the strength to open shot him a merciless glare.

"That wasn't what I was going to say."

"What were you going to say?"

"The obvious, Suze. Where's the booze?"

She didn't wind down with the first glass of wine, but the second hit her faster than a bullet. Until then, Stix had bided his time, but on her return trip from switching on the news, he tossed two couch pillows onto the deep-pile carpet and motioned her to sit next to him.

Either the wine or his monklike behavior for the past three weeks had its effect. Without a word, she dropped down by his side with a sleepy-eyed yawn and a trusting smile.

"You like kids," he mentioned.

"Kids, yes. But as for those two precocious monsters upstairs . . ."

"You love 'those two precocious monsters upstairs.'"

"Hopelessly," she agreed.

"In fact, you're a total sucker for anything to do with family and a home and anybody shorter than four feet tall."

"Hey, leave me some pride." Susan sipped the last drop of wine from her glass and shook her head. "How does Kay survive the days?"

"Vitamins?"

"They adore you, too," Susan told him. "Don't you ever lose patience?"

"With a kid? No way."

She turned on her side, propping up on one elbow. "Is that how you were raised? Patience and noise and confusion, lots of hugs and kisses, endless cocoa?"

"No."

When he said nothing else, she reached over and poked a finger at his ribs—the most aggressive physical action he'd ever seen her make. "You are extremely stingy when it comes to talking about yourself, shorty."

"You think so?"

"I think so. Just because you have everyone else spilling their life stories, you have the town believing you're quite a talker. Brother, have you got them fooled."

Actually, Stix thought she was the one who was the expert at fooling people. For the past three weeks, he'd played it her way. "Just friends" was her creed and cause, so that's what he'd been—someone to take up the slack of a restless Saturday afternoon, someone to take the edge off a too-quiet Sunday morning. That was all she wanted, and to the whole damn world she projected the image of a self-sufficient lady who had absolutely no need of kisses.

He'd been a friend, but she no longer fooled him. He had never met a woman in his life who needed kisses more.

Her throat was long and white. Her waist had a nipped-in slimness. He liked the weight on her thighs that made her so constantly worried. He liked the snugness of her bottom in jeans. She was made the way a woman was supposed to be made: touchable, not breakable, with a little flesh where a man liked a little flesh, and a soft small mouth that could rip a man's sanity from here to Siberia.

His sanity had been taking that round trip from Siberia for weeks now. She was too damned alone. Sass and humor kept her out of trouble. She was very good at keeping out of trouble, but even a self-contained rock had more needs than food, shelter and a job. Her parents had been killed in a car crash when she was four, and her blithely told stories of being shuttled between foster homes had moved him. Susan had made her own way along some lonely, rocky roads and he was unspeakably proud of her.

He was also mad at her. She was a warm-blooded human woman. Too warm-blooded, too human, too generous and passionate, to be wasting every night in emptiness.

"What are you looking at?" she asked suspiciously.

"The small scar right at the hollow of your throat." He traced the tiny white line.

She shivered suddenly, and tensed like a cat. He could have predicted that her voice tone would change from sleepy-warm to husky and whiskey-dry. "Just an accident with a broken piece of glass about a thousand years ago, and don't change the subject. You were about to tell me your entire life history—beginning with trike accidents and moving into where you were born, how many people were in your family. You know, all those details you're usually so stingy with. I'm positive you can talk if you try. I know you have functioning vocal chords.''

He noted that his slightest touch—in this case fingertip to throat—made her chatter like a VCR tape on fast forward. Talking, for Suze, was a wonderful, effective, distracting defense that he'd seen her exercise with regular success on countless occasions. Poor Susie. She had no idea he was on to her.

Instead of pulling back, he leaned closer and let his hand drift into her hair. The fine strands curled around his fingers, the pulse in her throat jumped, and faster than bad news, he had more conversation.

''It helps to talk, you know. If not to me, darn it, then to someone. I think it might help if you at least tried to talk about it, Stix.''

''Talk about what?''

''You know what. Kay.''

He knew he was getting to her when she brought in her frontline defense. She trusted that three-letter name the way a general trusted a Sherman tank. She'd done it before—brought up Kay's name—and before, he had immediately withdrawn faster than the slam of a bullet. That was what he was supposed to do. That was what he instinctively did. That was what she expected him to do.

''Not this time, Suze,'' he said softly.

''Pardon?''

"You keep knocking at that door." His thumb nudged her chin up so he could see her eyes. "You're that positive you know what's on the other side?"

Four

Susan had no idea when the lamp-bright living room had turned into a minefield. She seemed to have volunteered for trouble when she brought up Kay, but that was illogical. Reliable as Christmas on December 25, at a mention of Kay's name Stix would back off, move a physical distance, shutter the emotion in his eyes.

This time, something had malfunctioned in the system.

Instead of backing off, he'd moved so close that she could see a night beard softening his chin. Instead of establishing physical distance, he was deliberately sifting her hair through his fingers. And instead of shuttering the emotion in his eyes, his gaze was intense, clear and ruthlessly focused on hers.

The way he looked at her made her heart pick up with stunning speed. "We're in Kay's living room," she remarked cheerfully.

"I know exactly where we are, Suze."

"The children could wake up any second." Her tone celebrated the possibility.

"They could."

"And Kay and Mitch could be home at any time. In fact, I think I heard something, didn't you? Maybe it was their car."

"It wasn't their car." He smiled, just a little one. So little that she wanted to remind him about his wonderfully safe reputation with women. "Am I doing something to make you nervous?"

"Don't be silly. I'm never nervous." The devil smiled harder, and his palm slowly slid down the slope of her shoulder. Her vocal cords constricted. "I don't suppose you're in the mood to take a brisk walk in the subzero temperatures outside?"

"No."

"I think—I *really* think—the fresh air would do you good."

He didn't seem to be listening. Her head was resting on a couch pillow. He stole it. Sometime recently she'd crossed her arms under her chest. He patiently uncrossed one and then the other, with the sole goal of winding her arms around his neck.

No one talked for the eternal span of a minute, then she started again. "All right, shorty. You're in the mood," she said humorously. "If you want a kiss, take a kiss. I'm just warning you you're going to feel embarrassed afterward. It's not me you want and it's not this you want from me. You had a little wine—"

Stix knew better than to wait for Susan to wind down. Susan wound up, not down, when she was scared.

He'd learned other things about her in the past three weeks. Because she was touchy about casual contact, his

mouth covered hers with intense, serious thorough-
ness, so she could make no mistake that this was casual. He kissed her once, then a second time. Then he
paused to lavish more serious attention to the scent of
her skin, the glow of lamplight on her hair, the sound
of her breath catching. His lips rubbed against hers
again. Rubbed, then teased. Teased, then took. Again.
Again.

An interesting little sound escaped from the back of
her throat, but Stix was not diverted. He had something to show Susan, something that wouldn't wait,
something that couldn't take place in a more ideal setting than Kay's living room.

No other woman had a mouth with the exact same
shape, size and texture as Susan's. He wanted—
needed—her to know that. He was kissing *her*. He
wanted to be certain she understood that there was no
possible way he ever had or could mistake her for another woman—not Kay, not anyone. He'd wanted to
tell her the afternoon of the football game, only he
hadn't known how.

He'd never been good with those kinds of words.
He'd never been good at *showing* a woman how he felt,
either. But this was different. This wasn't about him.

It was about Susan, and because he couldn't talk, he
showed her that he found her mouth incomparably
special, her tongue one of a precious kind. She had a
spray of freckles on her nose to kiss, that pattern un-
duplicated in anyone else. Her throat needed attention.
No one had a long white throat quite like Susan's.

Momentum built from instinct. Maybe he was a little rough. He was awfully tired of her bringing up Kay.
He knew damn well she had it ingrained in her head that
he carried the emotional baggage of another love.

Maybe he did. Maybe he didn't. The only thing he knew with absolute certainty was that at this moment, this night, this woman with the pale, bruised mouth and the vulnerable dark eyes mattered to him in a different way than anyone else ever had.

She murmured his name, both a call and a protest. "Listen," she whispered.

"Shh." He was learning things he needed to know, wanted to know. She loved having her thigh stroked. She shivered all over when his mouth nuzzled into the neck of her sweater, where the skin was soft, white, warm. His fingers pleated on her breast, then scissored closed into a palm that kneaded and stroked. She came apart at that caress; he had to gather her, length to length.

She liked leaning length to length. Yielding and supple, she curled around him. She smelled like peaches and wine, and her mouth finally tasted willing—wild and abandoned and willing. Their tongues dueled. Both won.

This close to fire, a man could burn up and not care. He wanted Suze naked. Now. Ten miles from civilization, nowhere near bright lamps and a distant television, and intimately close to a mattress. Heat tensed already taut muscles. Desire lit through his bloodstream like flame. His hands weren't as steady as they should be—as he wanted them to be.

When Susan turned liquid, she could make a man forget time and place. He wanted total awareness, not the thick swamp of his own needs. For all her fast talking, she'd never told him the things he was learning now.

He'd assumed her sophistication; he was finding her innocence. Her hands clutched and spread, roaming his

shoulders and back as if she weren't sure what to do
with them, as if being loved and wanted and cherished
were a surprise. When his blue jeaned thigh rubbed between hers, he felt a tremor like fear shake her, then a
trembling like shyness. He knew damn well she'd made
love before because she gave, in kisses and touches. She
knew how to give, but an open invitation to take—and
she lost all confidence and certainty.

Susan wasn't at all familiar with feeling good about
Susan.

For an annoying moment there was a draft of cold
air, the low buzz of voices. He lifted his head long
enough to deliver a firmly snapped, "Good night,
Mitch. Good night, Kay." His eyes never left Susan's
face and then his mouth dipped down again.

"Stix—"

"Shh."

"Was that—?'

"Shh."

Susan wasn't in some dream. She saw no mist and
roses. Bela Lugosi was waving a cape on the television;
the rough nap of the carpet was unyielding. She had all
her clothes on. He had all his clothes on. She had
enough grasp of reality to know that nothing...
irretrievable...was happening.

Except that she seemed to have temporarily mis-
placed all her common sense. And all of her heart.

His mouth made love to her mouth, then he wreathed
a necklace of kisses around her throat and she thought
damn you, damn you....

Her response to him wasn't simple. Needs never were.
His embrace in the football stadium had given her a
glimpse of a lonely, hungry man. His embrace now took
her further, offering her images of what Stix could be

as a lover—with a woman he truly loved. He'd pent up emotion for so long. He'd deprived himself of passion, the comfort and lure of being held, the treasure of tenderness, the champagne soar of desire. Ghosts weren't keeping him warm: he needed someone.

And he kissed her as if he were just discovering that— explosively. He kissed her like a man coming alive. He kissed like she mattered. Like the world could go to hell. Like time had just started with the two of them. Like...

She tore her mouth away, breathing hard. Her eyes squeezed closed. *Get yourself together, Susan Markham. Do it now and do it fast.* This was Kay's living room and Kay's house, the last place she should have allowed herself to be caught up in illusions. For all she knew, the setting could have caught Stix up in his.

"Suze?"

The sleepy, dazed look in his eyes didn't do a thing for her peace of mind. She bolted up, springing free. She was still breathing hard, but now it shamed her. Talking—fast—was the easiest way she knew to regain control. Chattering six for a dozen, she retucked her sweater, switched on three lamps, turned off the television and refluffed every pillow in the living room.

"Talk about your swept-away technique, shorty! We're going to have to patent you under Dangerous Substances if this ever happens again. Heavens, look at the time. You have to be up in just a few hours. I'll take care of these glasses—"

She took care of the glasses. "Now what did Mitch do with our jackets? Look, Stix, I don't want you worried about this. Hormones can get away from anybody. Nature set that up with a guarantee. Believe me, I never thought you planned anything, and I certainly hope you don't think I—"

She saw the brick-wall chest coming toward her. "Shut up, Suze," he said gently. "Try and calm down, would you? Nothing happened."

"I *am* calm and I *know* nothing happened."

His palms cradled her face and he kissed her once, hard, then moved away. "I'll get our jackets, and I'm driving you home."

He couldn't have unnerved her more if he'd shaken her. His voice was low and calm and his kiss, brief. But his touch had been dominatingly possessive and his dark gaze intimate, knowing, caring. Where was his laid-back grin? Where was his slough-off laziness when she needed it? Where was the Stix she knew? "You can't drive me home. We both drove, remember? I have my own car."

He brought her jacket from the front-hall closet, murmured a raw, impolite verb in reference to his car and repeated, "So we leave my car and take yours, but like I said, I'm driving you home. I'm also going to see you to your door. And I'm probably going to kiss you again before I let you go inside, alone, to lock all your careful bolts. Try arguing with me, Susan."

She did try. There was no arguing with him about cars, but on the drive home, she blurted out something about bonds—the kind of fragile, special bonds two people form who understand each other.

"I'm not presuming what you feel, Stix, and on the surface, I had an entirely different experience than you did. I was involved with a man who was trying to forget someone else, a man who assumed he could force someone else to substitute for his first love. But the results were the same. I loved someone who wouldn't, or couldn't, love me back. So have you. I think that's why we formed a bond from the first. I value the friendship; I value the right to talk to you, to find someone who's coming from the same place, the same set of rules, the same understanding of bridges that neither of us want crossed.''

She kept talking. It could all have been summed in four words—*please don't hurt me*—but she laced the message in length and tact and gentleness because she didn't want to hurt him.

If he didn't verbally respond, she knew he heard her. He'd focused intensely on her words when she mentioned the man she'd been involved with.

She thought he understood. She'd give him absolutely everything she had and could as a friend, as long as they both drew the line at physical intimacy—but in the shadow of her porch, Stix showed a streak of macho Marlboro man. All men, of course, had a touch of that appalling nonsense, but she'd thought better of him. She'd also thought better of herself. For a brief moment she was plastered against the door as though she was the floor and he were the rug. His kiss was angry, thorough, and devastatingly passionate. And he left her with an ominously gentle "We'll talk tomorrow, Susan. Believe it."

He never called her Susan and *she* had already talked. Stix had abruptly, unfairly, unreasonably turned deaf, and she locked herself inside the house, feeling shaky and troubled.

She didn't know what he had in mind for tomorrow, but she swiftly knew what she did.

At three o'clock the next afternoon, Susan was enclosed in a pitch-black womb. Her spine was impaled on a wall of rock and her cleated boots clamped to the opposite wall. Her thighs and calves were tense enough to make her want to scream. She edged her feet down five inches, then moved her spine, then her feet, then her spine again, in a technique every caver called "chimneying." She called it torture. *Are you out of shape or what, Susan Markham?*

Twenty-five feet down she touched terra firma. "All right, Johnny, your turn," she called up. "Take it slow, and watch for a sharp edge on the north wall."

The distance from Moscow to good mountain and cave country was several hours' drive. As Susan had learned a long time ago, though, distances could be measured in both the physical and the psychological.

Her intellectual interest in caves had always had an emotional side. Here was another world. Above ground, the snow was burning bright and the wind was a raw, biting, bitter cold. In any cave, all sense of weather, time and season disappeared. The temperature rarely varied from fifty-five degrees, and the stillness and silence below ground were absolute.

She knew the chamber room she dropped into because she had been there before. Turning slowly, she let her carbide helmet light wander the open space—roughly eight feet by twelve, and big for the caves in this area. Unhooking the thermos chained to her belt, she dropped down to a squat, waited for Johnny and informed herself that this was one place she couldn't possibly think about Stix.

Johnny took ten minutes. Not to think about Stix during that time was impossible. Still, she was ready with a smile when her sixteen-year-old companion dropped to the ground next to her.

Johnny's forehead was beaded with sweat—so much so that she had to be careful not to smile. He was only sweating so hard because he was rigged up with rap-

pelling rack, aluminum-rung ladder, caver's backpack
and belaying hooks. All the equipment was as new as his
birthday. Absolutely none of it was necessary, but Susan would have bitten her tongue before raining on his
parade. She'd taken on novice spelunkers before, but
Johnny was a favorite.

"It's harder than I thought," he said wryly.

She nodded and handed him a tin mug of coffee.
"And all for few rewards. This cave's not exactly exciting, but that passage is unbeatable for practicing chimneying. You can take it up and down a few more times
before we leave, if you want."

"I'd rather use the ladder and rappelling hook."

"We'd all rather run before we walk," she teased
him, which earned her a grin.

He jerked off his fancy helmet, wiped his forehead,
and jammed the helmet back on. "You ever fallen, Susan?"

"A dozen times."

"You ever been caved in?"

"Once or twice."

"What's it feel like?"

She knew Johnny was referring to a literal cave-in,
but all she could think about was feeling caved-in—lost
and abandoned and blind in a man's arms the night before. "Petrifying," she said briefly, and changed the
subject. "You've been practicing your Prusik knots?"

"Sure. Want to see?"

Within seconds, he'd uncoiled his nylon rope,
crouched down, and started flaunting his new skill. The
technique was to create a knot that slid easily up the
rope, but locked when pressure was applied downward. The Prusik knot was a caver's staple, a potential
lifesaver, and Johnny needed to master it.

Unfortunately he had, which made it too easy for her mind to wander to a very different male—a man with a boyish shock of hair, soul-dark eyes and a mouth that could kidnap a woman's common sense.

"I'm going to chimney up and down a few more times if it's okay with you," Johnny said.

"Sure. Just remember the rough spot on the north wall. Anchor your spine to the west."

"I know that, Susan."

She closed her eyes, sipped at the bitter coffee and thought, I know a lot of things, too. The problem is that I forget them.

Drinking coffee wasn't taking up the slack; it just made her jumpy. She stood up, feeling restless and achy and angry with herself. Stix was dominating every mood, every thought, every action. She knew only one sure antidote for that disease, so she forced herself to remember Karn.

Karn had taught her a great deal—all she ever needed to know—about pain. Her geology professor had looked nothing like Stix. Karn was built stocky and stable; he had a thinning head of hair and several years on her. When she met him, she'd already had a lot of reasons to doubt her ability to love and to be loved.

The last thing she'd needed then was rejection. She had a childhood of heart-trampling memories to make her gun-shy, scared and wary going into the relationship. Perhaps because he was older, Karn was endlessly patient. He was also a special man, although his honesty and generous empathy alone would never have wooed her out of her glass house.

Karn needed her. No one had ever needed her before. That thrill of mattering, of being needed, was as heady as champagne and rainbows and hope. She'd known he'd lost his wife two years before she met him, and he'd admitted to having a tough time getting over his loss. She'd never been jealous when he occasionally called her by his wife's name instead of hers. She had never worried when he frequently brought up memories of his wife. She was glad he had those memories, and with the blind ego of the very young, blithely assumed that the "right woman" would help him put those memories in perspective.

She'd believed herself to be the "right woman," and by the first night he'd taken her to bed, she'd felt supremely loved and loving. That was not a night she was likely to forget. No one could be more naked and vulnerable than a first-time lover, and with passion and tenderness and desire he'd called a name, over and over, in the darkness.

Only it wasn't *her* name, but his dead wife's.

She'd crushed into more pieces than fragile crystal mowed down by a bulldozer. She never blamed Karn because he was never a deliberately cruel or insensitive man, just a human one. To her, the misspoken name was not the source of pain, but its symbol. He'd needed her; she'd failed. There was no question in her mind that he wanted to love her, that he had tried to love her.

From the time your parents died, Ms. Markham, I believe a good number of people have tried to love you. Why is it they always have to try so hard?

Is this a formal interview, sir?

Yes, Ms. Markham.

Well, then. The answer is . . . I don't know, I don't know, I don't know. . . .

"Susan? I've chimneyed up and down three times. Couldn't I try the rappelling hook now?"

She flipped the lid on the thermos and reattached it to her belt, her movements quick and impatient. She hadn't laid that old insecure nonsense on herself in a very long time. *What is the matter with you today?*

"Next time," she promised Johnny. "It's getting late and we still have a long drive home."

"Just once?" he coaxed.

She relented, then regretted it because she was stuck with another twenty minutes pacing the eight-by-twelve cave chamber with nothing else to do physically. She knew what was wrong with her today. It wasn't old memories, but new ones.

After Karn, she'd had the sense to pack it in. When every throw of the dice turned up snake eyes, one pulled up one's chips and quit the game. The poets could have love; she figured she'd worked on life. She had. Damn successfully.

Pushing at the heavy helmet covering her head, she rubbed her temples. Her life had seemed pretty darn good until she met Stix. Her being drawn to him was easy to understand. She saw Stix, like Karn, throwing away present chances of happiness because of a past love. She didn't want that happening to him. No one knew the power of ghosts more than she did. An empathetic friend could surely help him open emotional doors again....

Poppycock, Markham. You're so in love with him you can't see straight.

She squeezed her eyes closed and ached with fear. Knowing better didn't seem to help. The emotion had been sneaking up on her like a thief in the night. She'd loved Karn, but not like this. No one had ever made her feel loved, wanted, needed, cherished, not the way Stix made her feel when he touched her.

But she would never survive another naked night in the dark with a lover who needed to close his eyes so he could imagine she was someone else. Not if that lover was Stix.

And she couldn't survive another failure. Stix had real needs. Only a competent woman who was sure of herself—her sexuality and self-worth and her ability to love—could meet those needs. Susan was sure of nothing—except that she wasn't going to do anything that risked hurting the man.

She knew he was going to call. When a woman draped herself all over a man like Silly Putty, he always called. She was the one guilty of opening up that whole Pandora's box.

So it was obviously up to her to close it.

Stix knew the exact moment she entered the restaurant. Business was always heavy at six o'clock on Mondays. No one wanted to make their own coffee on a dark, gloomy winter morning. Having breakfast out chased the Monday-morning doldrums and gave people a chance to share lies about their weekend. But that's not why you're here, Susan Markham.

She shed her coat at the door. Sal tried to seat her, but Susan shook her head. Stix caught a quick glimpse of her red-and-white striped blouse and red skirt and her jaunty step swinging toward him, but then he was stuck. Bits of ham, potato, onion and cheese had to be folded into the omelet. The grill had three going and orders for four more. With George out sick, he didn't have a prayer of getting even three seconds free for the next two hours.

Just before the edges of the omelet bubbled, he turned his head again. Sal was still trailing her, but she'd stopped to glance around. He wondered what she'd think of his diner. It wasn't fancy. The blue hanging lamps matched the carpet, not because Stix gave a hoot about matching anything but because he'd always figured people didn't need screaming colors first thing in the morning. Some said he'd made a go of the place because he was perceptive about what people needed.

He wished to hell he knew what Susan needed. The question had clawed at him all Sunday, particularly when he'd stopped by her house and found her gone at ten—and noon, and two, and six.

He had to turn back. The omelets were past the bubble-edged stage. Yesterday, he'd made the best omelets in town.

"I hear you're a little short staffed this morning, shorty."

Her soft brown eyes were full of life, full of dance. His narrowed, not because she had stolen a slice of bacon but because her smile was too easy, too natural. Laid-back was his style, not hers. "Missing a cook and a busboy—but surviving. You have an early class on Mondays?"

She nodded. "An eight o'clock. And I was desperate. I came in to mooch free coffee." She patted his fanny. His back straightened like a poker.

The next thing he knew she was winging the glass pot of coffee around the counter, not to fill a cup for herself, but to refill his customers. She chatted to Harvey until the cop's uniform's buttons nearly popped. She listened to Rosie's Monday-morning woes. She was still hearing about Barker's weekend paneling project when he caught her picking up a hot pad.

Patiently he removed the hot pad from her hand and replaced it with a mug of caffeine. For those bare seconds when his hand touched hers, his heart beat parade rhythms. She tossed him the blithest smile he'd ever seen.

All right, Suze. You tore me inside out Saturday night. Now what are you up to? Stix asked her silently.

"I can handle a hot pad, you know. And if push comes to shove, I can even fry an egg," she murmured. "You could use some help. The place is packed."

"So sit down somewhere where I can see your crossed legs."

She glanced down at the limbs displayed below her scarlet wool skirt. "Like them?"

"'Like' is a pale word. Those legs are heavy breathing material."

"You have disgracefully easy standards. I've always liked that quality in a man. Where do these pancakes go?"

"On a plate—here—where Sal will pick it up in about thirty seconds. You go—" he scuttled a stool closer to the grill "—right here."

But she didn't sit. She breezed around him for spare napkins. She repoured coffee for the insatiable counter crew. She swiped at Formica tops. She met Sal and Amy and the busboy. She watched Mrs. McCarthy and Julie and Angie Davis come in, and if she noticed, he didn't hug any of them. They all looked as if they definitely needed a Monday-morning hug. He acted as virtuously as a reformed ex-con.

She didn't seem to notice. She was too busy driving him out of his mind. Her palm skidded over his spine in passing. Two more times, she patted his fanny. She whispered an outrageous comment that made him burn three eggs. Her hip bumped his when she scooped up a plate of biscuits. There went the toast.

And then she was gone.

"Stix?"

He focused blank eyes on Mrs. McCarthy's wrinkled smile. "Cat got your tongue this morning, honey? I wanted to thank you for making my waffles just the way I like 'em. Nobody else takes the time for an old woman. You sure I can't adopt you?"

Mrs. McCarthy asked him the same question every morning. He always had a ready answer for her. She counted on it.

His eyes skimmed under blue lights, over blond and brunette and red heads. The swinging legs were gone. The red-and-white striped blouse was nowhere in sight. Her coat had disappeared from the hook at the front, and yes, he knew what time it was—time for her to get to her eight o'clock class.

She'd only had a few minutes to make her point: Saturday night had been erased from the map. Latitudinal and longitudinal lines defined the boundaries of friendship. *Aren't we easy together? Aren't we comfortable? Everything's fine, shorty. Nothing that mattered happened.*

He thwacked a spatula against his palm. Frustration raised his blood pressure, and hurt sludged through his bloodstream.

Without a word—without giving him one chance to talk to her—she'd diminished Saturday night to a lost moment of insanity and let him off the hook of futures and commitments. There had been times in his life when he'd prayed for that kind of humor and tact. But that was after an awkward encounter with the wrong woman.

He'd never been told quite so gently, tactfully and thoroughly that he was the wrong man.

The headache thrumming in his temples warned him that maybe she was right. Maybe to wade into any deeper waters was to hurt Susan. He'd always carefully avoided hurting any woman before, knowing his feelings for Kay would sooner or later intrude; and the last person on this earth he wanted to hurt was Susan.

Dammit. He'd kill anyone who dared to hurt Susan.

Running a hand through his hair, he tossed down the spatula. The counter blurred in front of him. The word *kill* initiated the annoying problem of double vision. Even unsaid, the thought sounded melodramatic, silly, totally unlike him.

He had absolutely no violence in his soul, no heroic tendencies, no secret wish to play Errol Flynn. Some men relished the role of knight. He relished food, sleep, and peace. The old archaic concepts of fighting for a woman, aggressively pursuing her, protecting her from life's dragons and witches had always sounded to Stix like the makings of a horror story. He always figured he'd get laughed off the stage if he tried to say romantic things. He wasn't the type.

Susan didn't need him. She needed a hero type. Someone with a lot of energy and a hell of a lot of patience. Someone who could outthink and outtalk her, which was no small project. Someone who was stronger than she was, because Susan was extraordinarily strong, and someone who didn't listen but just loved her. And loved her and loved her and loved her. . . .

"Honey?"

Again, he raised his eyes for Mrs. McCarthy's rosy cheeks and kindly old eyes. "Do you have any aspirin?" he asked her.

Five

Until Susan zoomed into her driveway Tuesday night with a carful of groceries, she was certain she'd handled that restaurant visit well. Stix was a man of action, not words, so she'd tried to show instead of tell him how it had to be. She did care, but she wasn't going to risk hurting either of them by messing up a damn good friendship with any intimate complications. He never had to know there was anything more to her feelings.

If he'd gotten the message, however, he wouldn't be pacing her porch right now. And he wasn't on her porch for long. She'd barely pocketed her car key before he tugged open the passenger door and started loading his arms with grocery sacks. She caught his quick grin and a lazy "Hi, Suze" before she realized something was wrong. Not heavy-emotions/end-of-the-world wrong. This was more basic. This was touchingly serious.

Someone had stolen his jeans and sweatshirt. Someone had roped him down, given him a haircut and knotted a blue and gold tie at his throat. His navy slacks were paired with an ancient butternut-colored suede jacket that had only the faintest reek of mothballs.

For his sake, she didn't let him know how good he looked to her. She righteously warned herself to make the encounter quick, but she could hardly send him away in that shape. "Are you coming from a funeral?" she asked sympathetically.

He ignored that, which she understood since his concentration was focused on juggling three grocery bags. "Can you get the milk and the door, Suze?"

"Would you believe I can even carry one of those?"

"I'd better. You don't want to develop the arm muscles of a female wrestler." Halfway up the stairs, he shook his head. "You always buy bricks at the grocery store?"

He teased her when she couldn't find her key, and she must have said something to make him laugh but didn't know what. She hadn't been home all day, and the newspaper tried to trip her at the door. Then there were lights to switch on, her coat to put away, mail to throw on the counter, and nerves to settle down. *Look, I'm not glad you're here. I refuse to be glad you're here. You upset me every time I see you. I'm scared of what I feel around you. I really did amazingly well until you came along....*

As he propped open her refrigerator door with his knee and rapidly piled in lettuce and cheese and milk, he didn't look like a man who could upset anyone. His tie was already loosened. He'd abandoned his shoes at the door. And he plucked a small plastic bag from a grocery sack with a puzzled frown, as if he'd never seen a package of women's basic cotton panties before. "Suze, I've been thinking," he said seriously.

That was a sure lead into trouble if she'd ever heard one. Acid turned in her stomach while she took the panties and efficiently hid them under the two loaves of bread. At the same time she reached for the laundry soap, he discovered her bag of apples and pilfered one.

"Any other woman I know," he said between munches, "would have tried to make something heavy and involved out of what happened Saturday night. But not you."

"Nothing happened Saturday night," she reminded him swiftly.

"Sure it did." He piled nail-polish remover, deodorant, Bufferin, peach soap and strawberry shampoo all in one place on the kitchen table. He acted just as if he regularly unpacked groceries for women. "We came very close to making love. However..." He examined the brand of her vitamins, then plopped the bottle on the table with the rest. "Luckily we're both too smart to get...'swept away.' Wasn't that how you put it? Especially you, Suze."

She found herself clutching the jar of coffee, unable to remember where it went. At times he had a voice just like honey and rum, a throat-soothing burr that went down so easily a woman could be distracted. Susan wasn't distracted; she was wary.

He poked through her bottom cupboards until he found the canned goods, then hunkered down with her jars of spaghetti sauce. "I never understood how you picked up on my old feelings for Kay until you mentioned that man Saturday night. What was his name?"

She hesitated. "Karn."

So. Finally he had a name for the son of a so-and-so who'd made Susan feel so damn bad about herself. He took two cans of soup in his hands, his tone as winsome and mild as a spring breeze. "So I thought about your... Karn. Actually, what I thought about is that we're two of a kind. We've both been down a one-way road and hung up at a stop sign. And that's pretty rare. Finding someone you can talk to. Really talk to."

"Yes." She crouched down next to him, not because he was making a total disaster of her cupboard, but because she had a sudden fierce need to be near him. Never mind that he was feeding her own words back to her, and to heck with getting hurt. If Stix honestly needed someone to talk to...

"All I thought, and keep thinking, is that we seem to understand each other. Honestly understand each other. There's no need for pretenses or games. Not with you."

"I'm glad you feel that way."

"You're special, Suze. In a way no one has ever been special for me."

He said it so lightly that there was no excuse for the sudden lump in her throat. Nothing was going on here. She was holding a can of mushrooms. He was holding a can of onions. Ice cream was melting on the counter. It was just at that one instant when her knee touched his knee and she caught the dark vulnerability in his eyes. He wasn't looking at her as a friend. The voltage in the room should have caused a power outage.

Then a can of soup toppled. When she reached in, he lurched to his feet and the contact was broken. "So, seeing as we clearly understand each other, there's no reason on earth why you can't go to a poetry reading with me tonight, is there? Assuming we feed you first.

Good grief, didn't you buy more meat than this bare bird?''

''Poetry?'' She echoed, as if the word were a new one in her vocabulary. It wasn't, but her heart was still, inexplicably thumping so hard that she may have—*must* have—misheard him. Poetry? Stix?

''There's some woman going to speak at the university gallery. Seven-thirty. You like poetry, don't you?''

''Since when do you go to poetry readings?''

''What, did you think I was some kind of uneducated cretin? I'm hurt, seriously hurt, but not nearly as badly as you're hurting.'' He glanced at her, then quickly away. ''I don't believe you got all this stuff at the grocery store without picking up one decent cut of meat.''

Susan didn't believe he seriously wanted to go to a poetry reading, but to make any sense at all out of his visit, she went.

Two days later, she spotted him sneaking in during the last five minutes of her Thursday noon lecture. Without removing his jacket, he sat in the last seat in the last aisle. If he came to listen—which she doubted—she didn't mind his hearing the end of her talk.

''We're too used to thinking of our world, with our Judeo-Christian values, as the way things are everywhere. The truth is that we're the odd ones out. Less than one-fifth of human cultures practice monogamy. Four-fifths permit men to have several wives simultaneously. The only cultures where long-term relationships thrive are where men and women are economically dependent on each other. Romantic illusions about happily-ever-afters simply never hold up in the light of day.''

She wound up the lecture, answered questions, collected 125 essays, and tried to keep her eyes away from the man at the back of the room. She had no idea why he was here. But then she had no idea why he'd suffered through a poetry reading last Thursday when he clearly valued poetry on a level with thumbscrews.

He waited until the last student exited before he ambled toward her with his long, lanky stride. Pitiful, the way her heart started thudding. One would think she was deliriously happy to see him.

I wish you'd stayed home.

She had no problems when he wasn't around. When he wasn't near her, it was easy to remember Kay, easy to remember her own track record competing with ghosts, easy to remember her pride.

When he came close, all she could think of was his dark, gentle eyes, the way he made her laugh, the sizzle charging through her blood and that he was annoyingly, irritatingly, exasperatingly, totally lovable.

She really wished he'd stayed home, and she braced when he finally reached her.

"You give quite a lecture on love and life, Suze." He sounded amused, and he stole the heavy stack of essays from her arms before she could stop him. "You don't even try to pull your punches with the kids, do you?"

"Because I stress reality instead of fairy tales?" She ducked her head and reached for her reading glasses on the podium. His eyes were drifting over her face in a too-gentle, too-probing way, as if he were searching for a younger woman who'd once foolishly believed in all the fairy tales. "Something tells me you didn't come here to hear a lecture on serial monogamy."

"Actually, I came because I was desperate for help."

Desperate? With that dawdling grin? "What kind of help?" Once out of the lecture hall, she pushed open the double doors and aimed for her third-floor office.

"You don't have any more classes this afternoon, do you?"

Since he already knew she didn't have classes past noon on Thursdays, she didn't bother to answer. He didn't, either, until her books and briefcase and essays were mounded on her office desk. Then he began, "I'm in serious trouble—"

"Heavens. I hope you called the cops."

"Not that kind of trouble." He carefully closed the door as if he were a teenage kid needing to privately discuss a case of athlete's foot with his coach. The way he dragged his hand through his hair added to the image. Red streaked his cheeks. He cleared his throat again.

The darn man was determined to make her smile. She tried desperately not to. She even propped her glasses on her nose in an effort to look schoolmarm serious. "I hope you're not here to ask me any awkward questions about the birds and the bees."

"I wouldn't be bothering you for anything that trifling."

"Ah. We're talking big-time trouble."

He nodded. "I need a suit."

She was surprised. Somehow she'd expected something with a little more emotional impact. Still, she slipped off her boots, dropped to the desk chair, and supported her chin in her palms, prepared to be sucked in by his tale of woe.

His attire had been well chosen as props for his cause. Until he'd shed his jacket, she had no idea he was auditioning for the role of street orphan. His shirt was frayed and missing buttons. His jeans were patched at the knee and thigh. His denim vest had holes. He pointed out the holes, the patches, and the missing buttons with due gravity and boyish despair.

"Shameful," she concurred wryly.

"I know, I know. And now I've got this thing where I have to have a suit."

"Thankfully there are men's stores both at the mall and downtown."

"Susan, you are not taking this seriously," he accused her.

"I'm trying, but you're making it so hard."

"You don't understand," Stix said gravely. "Some men are afraid of heights. Give me a cliff. Just don't make me go in a store alone. We're talking a serious anxiety attack here. We're talking hopeless bad taste. We're talking no knowledge of styles. I didn't even know men were still wearing suits until this thing came up. I need help. I need advice. I need moral support. I need—"

He drawled out all those needs in winsomely buttered tones. She'd never heard a man so desperate, so earnest, so full of bull. *But I don't care, Mr. Stanley Nicholas Sperling. You're hopelessly lovable. I grant that. I even grant that I love you, but I'm not getting drawn in. Do you hear me?*

Unfortunately, as with the reasons behind the poetry reading, she couldn't get a straight answer out of him for love or money. Why was he *really* here? The question seemed basic enough. Only his record was stuck on suits, so she finally gave in and took the orphan shopping.

That proved an exercise in leading a horse to water with the last part of the adage holding the most true. "So, what size are you?"

"Size?"

He knew nothing. The neat racks of suits produced no flicker of recognition. It was like dealing with a child who'd been raised by the wolves. "You like navy? Gray? You want plain or a stripe?"

"Sure. Whatever you think."

She waved her hand in front of his eyes to make sure someone was home. "At least offer me a little basic guidance, shorty—like in the area of money. Are we dealing with cash? Credit cards? A budget-line item? How far were you planning to go into hock here?"

"The restaurant's solvent. You couldn't put me in hock."

"Trust me. Given a store and an open checkbook and I can put anyone in hock."

"You like shopping, don't you? I thought you would. I—" As if he'd just discovered his foot in his mouth, he clammed up and backed into a table of shirts. He plucked up one with purple and orange stripes. "Is this what men are wearing now?"

Alarmed, she removed the shirt. "Some men, yes. *Not* you."

"Yes, Suze."

The whole afternoon proved long and upsetting. Guilt was partly responsible for that. She'd been so certain that he had some sneaky, subversive, complicated reason for this outing that the truth startled her. He really did want a suit. Only that was easier said than done. Men with goalpost shoulders were tough to fit. Black made him look like Abe Lincoln. Pinstripes and vests made him look like a bohemian playing yuppie.

She knew the navy one was perfect the instant he dragged on the jacket, but that created a new problem.

He looked wonderful in navy. Edible. Elegant. Transformed from a huggably disheveled bear into a commanding, sexy, dominantly striking man, as tall as trouble and just as disturbing.

With the brilliance of hindsight, she knew she shouldn't have gotten into this. Sips of possessiveness kept creeping up on her like champagne on an empty stomach. A woman picking out a man's clothes implied certain rights. She didn't want those rights, and she went into a perfect frenzy over ties.

"They all look okay to me," Stix mentioned of the four displayed over her arm.

"We're not looking for okay. We're looking for ideal."

"I like the blue one with the little yellow tennis rackets."

She picked the red-and-blue stripe—Stix knew nothing, his opinion had been long dismissed between her and the salesman—and headed back to the shirt table. Solids? Stripes? Stix wasn't going to wear a suit that often. She didn't want him stuck with shirts that wouldn't work for any occasion.

As for Stix, well, he wasn't growing impatient, but in due time he scooped up the half dozen shirts under discussion and headed for the cash register. Susan paled as the clerk punched in the total.

"Lord! How did that happen? Listen, we could cut the shirts down to three. Maybe only take one of the ties—"

She was still protesting when he headed for the door. She had to open it because he was knee-deep and nose-high in parcels. Once on Main Street, they were immediately immersed in Arctic cold and attacked by home-scurrying pedestrians trying to mow them down. The sheer number of people on the sidewalk suggested it was five o'clock, which she knew was impossible. She would never have subjected Stix to four hours' nonstop shopping. Embarrassment hit her with the subtlety of a freight train, which he readily diverted when he started piling the packages into her arms.

"Hey!"

"Just hold them for a second, would you? I forgot something." The shirt boxes alone reached her throat, then came the sock bags, which totally blocked her vision—his goal. "I owe you dinner out for suffering through that with me."

"No, you don't, and no, I can't. I have a hundred and twenty-five anthro essays to grade tonight. Stix!" She felt her purse slap her coat side, but was more conscious of the whole cliff starting to tip. Seconds later, the mountain began to recede. One by one he reclaimed the packages, but something was wrong. His grin was all mischievous boy, but for that long moment his eyes were all man, vibrantly intense, disturbingly aware.

"I thought we had that straight."

"You thought we had what straight?"

"You don't have to use the 'grading tests' excuse. Not with me. A simple no will do just fine. I thought you understood you could be honest with me, and grading some tests or essays is not the reason you turned down dinner." He didn't give her a chance to answer before his voice lowered and softened. "You turned down dinner, Suze, because you were scared. Honest scared. Gut scared. Because we both know something could happen if we're not careful."

She stared at him. He hadn't taken the words right out of her mouth, but stolen them, ruthless as a robber, directly from her heart.

"I'm *not* going to hurt you. Would you try to believe that?"

Watching him walk away, she didn't know what she believed. Except that he was right. She *was* scared. Honest scared. Gut scared. And every minute she spent with him, the emotion was growing, faster than a brushfire and just as uncontrollably.

You can be honest with me, Suze. It was eight o'clock on Friday, a week after their talk about honesty. The sky was a star-studded black and the roads an ice rink by the university auditorium. *Honesty, my foot. Wait until I get my hands around your neck, Stanley Nicholas Sperling.*

Susan eased out of the Rabbit's driver's seat, frozen to her toes. Her black velvet cape was good for show, not warmth, and her full-skirted white silk dress did a fantastic job of covering her thighs but invited drafts in embarrassing places. She entered the double doors of the theater with a crowd and prayed she would unthaw before June.

A dozen people stopped to talk to her while she frisked her black beaded bag for her ticket—the same ticket that Stix had sneakily, furtively and *dishonestly* stuffed into her purse the day she'd taken him shopping. After handing in the ticket, she surged toward the warmth of the theater proper. Her seat was 2-B, as in second row, second seat in, and provided an unbeatable view that was about to be wasted on her.

Cultural events were regularly offered between the neighboring universities at Pullman and Moscow. Susan often took advantage of them, but her taste ran toward the annual Moscow Sci-Fi Convention, not ballet. Not that the visiting Russian performers weren't a rare treat for a classical music fan, but what could she do? She was born loving rhythm and blues.

At the moment, draping her cape over the seat, she felt as if she'd been born cold. She sneaked a peak at the mirror in her purse. Thankfully, her mascara hadn't frozen and her numb lips still had a fancy coating of red. For once, her hair was even behaving.

She tucked the purse at her side, fussed with the white silk draping at her throat, checked that her earrings were on straight, and crossed her legs. Then uncrossed them. Then recrossed them.

She wasn't nervous. She looked her absolute best. A woman who looked her absolute best was never nervous. Tearing-one's-hair-out confused was a completely different emotion.

As the lights dimmed and the violins warmed up, her pulse drum-rolled the arrival of 2-A. Quieter than a whisper, the man in the dark navy suit and the navy-and-red striped tie dropped into the next seat. She caught a warm whiff of after-shave when he turned his head. His gaze drifted over her with the casual indifference of a stranger. That didn't last. His whistle was low and wicked and had a lot in common with the man.

"Hi, Suze."

She wasn't going to melt for that "Hi, Suze." Not this time. "Since when, Mr. Sperling, did you become a ballet enthusiast?"

"Surprise you?"

She meant to answer, but all light died and the performance began. A dozen ballerinas flowed across the stage, graceful and skilled enough to convert even a hard-core rhythm-and-blues fan. She would have watched with far more concentration if she hadn't had to keep her eye on Stix. He had a problem finding a place for his knees. He had a problem with a tight tie. He had a problem trying to hunch his shoulders so that the woman in back of him could see.

She waited twenty minutes before demurely murmuring, "Aren't they fantastic?"

"Riveting," he whispered back.

"You're really enjoying the performance, aren't you?"

"Very much. Always loved ballet."

Like the plague, he loved ballet. Minutes later, she caught him stifling a yawn, and would have laughed out loud if she hadn't felt so smotheringly frustrated.

She knew exactly why she was here. She was crazy, that was why. The worst weakness she had, the one she'd never mastered, the only one she'd never been able to control, was the need to be needed. With Stix, gray days turned to technicolor. Wants shimmered. Yearnings whispered. And he usually seemed so darned happy to be with her that she was drawn into the illusion that he needed—not someone, not anyone—but her.

But those were her problems. She knew what to do with her problems, but she didn't know what to do about his. Recently Stix had done a lot of chanting about no-strings friendship and honesty. That was fine. He talked the exact game—the only game—she was willing to play. But then came the poetry reading. And the shopping. And now, the ballet.

The man sitting next to her concealed a second yawn.

Ten minutes later she heard his knee crack when he tried to silently shift his long leg into the aisle.

The violins were just reaching a tragically emotional crescendo when she saw his hand sneaking toward his mouth for yet a third time. Quicker than the spring of a mousetrap, she grabbed his wrist and reached back for her cloak. "All right. That's it! Come on, shorty," she whispered darkly.

"What's wrong?"

"Shh." She sent a dozen telepathic apologies to the performers and did her best to tiptoe up the dark aisle. It wasn't easy to tiptoe in high heels, and harder yet to be innocuous towing a six-foot-six giant. Once through the double doors, they found themselves in the softly lit and empty lobby.

"Susan? Are you ill? What's wrong?"

"I'm not ill and everything's fine." She dropped his hand long enough to pull on her cloak, and then muttered, "Or almost everything. Damn! I forgot my purse." She glanced up to see his mouth twitching.

She wanted to be angry with him. She was almost positive she was angry with him. He'd caused her sleepless nights. She felt uncomfortable around a man she didn't understand, and she certainly didn't understand Stix. But there was that grin. A playing-hookey, crookedly fervent "Thanks, Suze, for getting me out of prison" grin.

"Darn it! Then why on earth did you buy the tickets?" she murmured helplessly.

"Pardon?"

"Nothing. Just... We're leaving. My car. Your house. And you're driving. I hate driving on ice."

"What about your purse?"

"Anyone that desperate to steal a black beaded bag containing a vial of perfume and a lipstick can have it. Otherwise I'll claim it from the Lost and Found tomorrow." She motioned him firmly toward the door. Happy as a truant, he headed out.

"But your car keys? Didn't your purse have your car keys?"

"This is no time to be practical." Once outside, she inhaled the first lungful of black, ice-bitter air and shuddered. "Of course my purse had my car keys, but that's nothing lost. A long time ago I learned to plant spares everywhere from the hood to the gas tank."

Twenty minutes later, Stix parked in the drive of his pine-hidden brick ranch. Seconds after that, they were inside. He took off her cape, turned on a lamp and silently mouthed "I'll make coffee" before disappearing into the kitchen.

She stared at his retreating back, thoroughly irritated with him. He'd undoubtedly mouthed the comment about coffee because he couldn't sneak a word in, dominantly making her aware that she'd prattled for the entire drive like a nervous goose. All men hated women who chattered. Why didn't he?

Stix might have patience to spare. She had none, especially with herself. Crossing her arms, she prowled his living room. The single lamp he'd switched on created more shadows than light, but she could see enough.

She'd expected a bachelor pad. Instead, she found a saddle-leather couch, overstuffed chairs and a hand-carved teak coffee table. He liked tobacco and copper colors, although his framed oils had splashes of apricot. He'd obviously built the teak cabinets for his sound system. The thick cream carpet was a sinfully delightful extravagance. He was neat. As a woman, she had a merciless eye for detecting a man who expected to be picked up after.

The look of the room raised a dozen questions about how little she knew Stix—where he'd come from, who he was, what he valued. She had the fleeting intuition that there were giant gaps in what she knew about him—things that mattered, but that had to wait. His room upset her on an entirely different, emotional level.

Her finger trailed the bare, varnished surface of his corner desk. She peeked into the round-arched stone fireplace, empty of ash and even dust. The copper magazine rack had nothing in it.

It took more time than money to create a room of comfort. Stix had spent both, and the proof was an absolutely lovely interior. This was a man who knew what a home was. He just didn't live here.

Damn you, Stix. Did he have to be lonely? Did the whole room have to shout it? Did she have to feel this fierce wave of protectiveness wash over her that tasted terribly annoyingly like love?

When she turned, she found him leaning in the kitchen doorway, his jacket off, his tie loosened. The look in his eyes did nothing to calm her brazen blood pressure. "What are you doing with your shoes still on, Suze? And coffee's ready."

She ducked under his arm and found his kitchen more of the same: a square room of attractive lemon and oak and dark-glassed appliances. But the surfaces were all clean, the cupboards and drawers all closed.

It was the drawers that got to her. Everyone left drawers hanging an inch or two open except saints, Julia Child, and men who were never in their kitchens long enough to make a little mess. Stix loved food. He knew how to cook and this was a marvelous kitchen to cook in. The refrigerator didn't have a single fingerprint. Darn it, wasn't he even eating?

"Want your coffee, Suze?"

"Yes," she said brightly, took the mug from his hands, set it on the counter and forgot it. She threw her hands in the air in a gesture of total despair. "What am I going to do with you?" she demanded.

Six

We have a problem?'' Stix asked her.

"You bet your sweet patooties we have a problem." But her first problem was feeding him. The longer she thought about it, the less she could remember the last time she'd seen him eating.

Stix without food was like a ship without barnacles: unnatural and distressing. She moved him aside and opened his refrigerator. Seven items were lined up on his counter in no time. Bad cooks were usually the most creative sandwich makers. "The problem, shorty, is that you hate poetry, despise shopping, and would rather get a cavity filled than attend a ballet." She foraged through his drawers until she found a butter knife. Once she found one, she shook it at him. "Nobody forced you into that stuff. You brought it all on yourself. That's exactly what makes no sense. Now, what are you doing, shorty?''

At the moment Stix was standing in the doorway trying to look inconspicuous. She wanted answers. Now. He tried hard to think of some, but mostly he was busy looking at her.

The cold air had burned a delicate coral into her cheeks and whitened the rest of her face to porcelain. Gold dangled from her ears. Her eyes were soft, luminous, distressed. She looked pretty silly spreading mayonnaise in white silk, but she also looked elegant, classy, feminine—and fragile. Susan was the most fragile woman he knew, although he expected she'd try to bat him across the room if he dared tell her that.

"You didn't like the poetry reading?" He tested carefully.

"What I like is not the point here. The point is that *you* don't—at least the kind of romantic poetry that reeks of hearts and flowers. So why did we go?"

"Didn't you like it?" he persisted.

"Yes."

She sounded so irritated that he had to be careful not to smile. "I know you like shopping."

"I never said I didn't." She aimed an enormous three-decker sandwich at him like a weapon—or as if she were positive he was starving. For the first time in ages, he was. "Actually, it's not that I like shopping; it's that my mother probably timed her labor pains between sales. It's in the genes, nothing I can fight."

"No one's asking you to fight it, Suze. And didn't you like the ballet? I thought all women liked ballet."

"But that's just it!" She shoveled all the sandwich-making supplies back into the refrigerator. "Why were you doing all this stuff for me? Since when have I ever given you the impression that I expect a friend to go through a lot of torture, sacrifice and suffering on my account?''

He swiped at a dollop of mayonnaise on his lip. ''Now, it wasn't that bad,'' he murmured dryly. ''Well, I admit the ballet verged right up there on borderline—''

''Stix, would you stop giving me a hard time? Talk to me. No frosting, no frills. Just tell me what's on your mind.''

He couldn't do that. If he honestly told her what was on his mind, he figured she'd run for the hills. No question she was slightly touchy on the subject of Kay.

So was he and always had been. But in trying to understand Susan, he'd forced himself to wade into some old, painful deep waters. For years he'd assumed his feelings for Kay hadn't changed, and with good reason. Any time he'd tried to form a serious attachment for a woman, those feelings had intruded.

For Stix nothing, precisely, had changed now. In fact, the more he was around Susan, the more he remembered the emotions that had drawn him to Kay: a deep and wholesome ache and pure specialness, a feeling strong and powerfully male and nurturingly protective. He'd never failed to feel good around Kay.

Susan certainly never gave him that problem. Around her, frustration, tension, confusion, slams of inadequacy and mountains of lust were the order of the day. As far as he could tell, she'd been put on this earth to destroy his life. He'd given up trying to sleep. His appetite was going. In the shower, he found himself weaving wild, exotic, erotic fantasies involving a very bare bed and an even barer Susan.

Kay had been easy on a man's mind. She still was. She had unconditionally accepted who he was as a man and a friend. She still did.

Suze accepted nothing. She nitpicked over his "swept away" technique, misunderstood his affectionate nature and nipped at the man's most secure values. She couldn't wait for him to do something wrong. Hell, he couldn't even kiss her without her leaping to the conclusion that he was using her. And look at her now. A guy tried to do a few subtle things to let her know he found her damn special. And what did he get? The third degree.

Loving Kay had been so restful.

He dusted the sandwich crumbs from his hands, aware that Susan was becoming tap-foot impatient. He thought of a hundred less difficult women he'd known. Why did this one have to make his blood spit and sizzle?

"So..." he drawled genially. "Are we all through with this discussion?"

She blinked. "All through? Stix, you haven't even started to talk!"

Of course he hadn't started to talk. Talking with Susan was like a novice poker player hoping he could win in Vegas. "What size shoe are you?"

"Pardon?"

"Never mind. It's a cinch you're no thirteen, so we'll have to work on socks. Three, four pairs of wool socks and you're bound to fit into a pair of my boots." He headed for the back hall, then turned around with a grin. "Ever gone sledding in the dark?"

Within an hour, he had an old-fashioned varnished toboggan at the top of a hill. Susan had tried, over the

same past hour, to interject sanity into the man. He'd
been too busy transforming her into the abominable
snowman to listen. Her white silk dress was now stuffed
beneath his fisherman's sweater. She was also wearing
his four pairs of wool socks, his boots, hat, scarf, gloves
and snowmobile suit—rolled four times at the cuffs.

"I was trying to talk to you. Do you remember? Talk.
It's something two people frequently do. One person
asks a question. The other person answers it. Didn't you
know? Communication is an extremely common way
for people to avoid misunderstandings—"

"You want the front or the back?"

"It is freezing," Susan continued patiently. "I have
no idea who owns this hill and it's past one in the
morning. We are probably going to get arrested."

"Okay for you. I was going to be a gentleman and
offer you the front, but heck. If you trust me to steer."

She opened her mouth one more time, then closed it.
A scrub brush wouldn't scrape off his grin; he was that
happy. What could she do? The man was demented.
She loved him happy.

But nobody steered her toboggan. At her fastest pace,
which was waddling, she slid down into the front of the
sled with her legs crossed under the curl. Susan, this is
not logical behavior, warned a small voice in her head.
The warning was unfair. The minute she glanced down
she very logically remembered her life insurance.

The view below could have been a visual advertise-
ment for Dramamine. Hills abounded in and around
Moscow, many of them gently rounded. Stix had chosen probably the only one with the killer death drop.

Oh, God! It wasn't just the death-drop hill that
caught her imagination, but the whole night. House
chimneys showed over the hills, but the valley tucked

between was as untouched as a virgin. The sky was a deep ebony, and even their breath seemed to puff a magical silver. The long, moonlit slope of snow had the dips and curls and shine of whipped egg whites. About a zillion miles straight down was a mystically shadowed cache of thick black pines.

Susan was uncharacteristically almost charmed by the fantasy of fairy-tale beauty. Until she took another good look at those pines. The ones right in their path.

"When this is over, I'm buying you your own private monogrammed straitjacket," she told Stix.

"Close your eyes."

She didn't. He pushed off before leaping onto the back. His weight alone propelled their downward momentum to what felt like bobsled speed. Snow stung, and wind lashed her cheeks more sharply than a whip. The toboggan ate up the white in a stomach-roiling, silent blur—silent until she heard laughter catching in the night, gaining in volume like a snowball. Damn, it was fun! "Lean right!" she screamed.

He leaned left, and since his arms were around her waist, he took her with him. The next thing she knew she was eating snow, the toboggan was angled straight up in the branches of a pine tree several feet away, and she was plastered all over a heavily breathing Stix. She raised her head to find him grinning.

"Didn't you realize? If we'd leaned right, we would have missed that tree," he mentioned.

"That was the idea, you turkey."

"Suze." He shook his head despairingly. "There are obviously major holes in your education. Don't you know anything about sledding? Crashing is half the fun." He pushed to his feet, shedding pounds of snow in the process. "Never mind. We'll give you another chance. Only this time let's work up a little speed."

"I'm quite sure we were already traveling at death-defying speeds."

"You innocent. You thought that was fast?"

The trek back up the hill was exhausting, but they did it three times. Once Stix took the front, but that was no good—she fell off halfway down the hill. The second time he lay flat on his stomach with her on his back holding on for dear life. That time they achieved a pace that pleased him. They also missed the pines by a measurable half inch. The third time he got this idea they should go down backward, lying on their backs.

"No," she told him simply. That basic syllable had transcended cultures and history and language barriers forever. Everyone understood it. Vaguely she was aware that she should have used it for poetry readings and ballets, but even careful women occasionally fell off the emotional wagon. Going downhill backward was a much simpler issue of life and death.

"Come on, Suze."

Shameful, the way her blood thickened to honey at that coaxing "Suze." So much for life and death. She stalled. "Anybody ever tell you you have a latent dare-devil streak?"

"What can happen? It's just snow."

He splayed on his back with his arms stretched out like a snow angel's. She suffered a lot of fast suspicions when he motioned her to climb on top of him. His smile was too smug and she didn't trust the devil in his eyes, but worries of that kind were obviously silly: these were probably their last moments alive. There was a time to fuss about propriety and a time to drape herself as close to the man as she could get.

When he used a foot to push off, she buried her head in his snow-encrusted shoulder and clutched good and hard.

She felt his arms tighten around her, and then there was nothing. Just an exhilarating rush of speed, the keening wind, snow slapping her cheeks, and the moon blurring past.

The tip-over crash was inevitable. Its aftermath was not. In time she recovered her breath and discovered she was still alive but half buried in a white-powder hill. She needed to move. She *meant* to move, but for long seconds, she simply didn't.

Apart from her being covered in snow from head to toe, snow was melting and dribbling down her neck, and she had to be frostbitten from her nose to her navel. Until that exact moment, she'd known they were both insane. Now what terrified her was that she no longer felt insane.

She felt good. The night was black velvet, the air lung-crushingly sweet, the scent of pines, magical. She was no stranger to play or laughter—both had gotten her through every crisis in her life. But she couldn't remember ever feeling this free, this exuberantly high on being alive, this devil draw of precious happiness.

"You okay?" Stix crawled to her side and loomed over her, making a huge snowy shadow. He whipped off his glove and started brushing snow from her cheek. When he looked at her face—really looked—his voice hoarsened and softened and burred. "I never thought I'd see you with that look in your eyes, Susan Markham."

"What look?"

"I know you don't want to believe this, but you're not just asking. You're begging for trouble."

"I admire your imagination. The reality is that I have snow in my belly button and I think I lost your boot on that daredevil ride. My entire body has been re-formed in the shape of a snowdrift—"

"Suze? What do you think is going to happen if you give in to it?" he whispered.

She refused to answer that.

"Try it, honey. For me. There's no one here but you and me. Try it. Just once."

A moment of silence locked in time, and then slowly, hesitantly, she framed his face with her half-frozen hands, raised up and touched ice-numb lips to his. It was that "for me" that undid her. She owed him thank-yous, for magically creating the shine of an ebony night and the whipped-cream snow. For the laughter. For the sharing. For being the man he was.

Shadows started to intrude—shadows of Kay and shadows of self-worth crushed in the illusion of love before. But those warning instincts stayed slumberish and vague. There was no need for them. The best kiss she could offer him was little more than the mating of two icebergs. Tons of wet clothes and snow and cold made every movement awkward. There was no possible way to get into any trouble.

It seemed . . .

It seemed . . .

It seemed she was wrong. Terribly wrong. He responded so passionately to the slightest touch of her lips, and when he wrapped his arms around her she discovered all about the kind of cold that burned. The friction of his mouth moving over hers caused a fast meltdown. And his tongue was warm—mobile and wet-warm and making a dive into darkness.

Sabotage came from within, not without. His cold cheek rubbed hers. He whispered something, then took her mouth again, and again. She saw the burn of longing in his eyes. She tasted need, raw and sweet and honest. His ice-cold fingertips touched her face, and she was suddenly reaching for him, not to take but to hold, not in selfishness but in giving.

Maybe her shifting weight caused the avalanche. Later she would remember that fall as the moment she could easily have broken away. At the time, when she felt the snow sliding, she held him more tightly instead of letting go, and they both went tumbling. First her on top. Then him, then her, and when they finally coasted to a stop, startled laughter echoed from both of them. Laughter faded to a shared breathless smile, and again she had the chance to sever the mood. All she had to do was take that chance.

She couldn't. Instead, she kissed him—no excuses, no hesitations. Her legs scissored around him and her tongue sought his. Her bones turned liquid, not from the power of his response but from the power of hers. She loved him, not a little but a lot. Not for the moment but for the whole kahuna.

She hadn't forgotten Kay. For all she knew, he could have sledded with Kay in the dark, could be thinking of her right now. That mattered, but not now.

What mattered was that Stix was a warm, generous man who needed to be loved. She owed him this moment of honesty, for suffering through the ballet, for not saying one word when she made him try on a thousand suits, for bringing her all those cherry doughnuts that went straight to her thighs. She owed him more than a nightful of kisses. Never mind where his heart was. She knew how he made her feel, and it had been a very long time since anyone had made her feel wanted, not for sex or company or what she could do for them, but just because she was Susan.

"Susie..." When his mouth tore from hers, she saw his eyes in the darkness, grave and black. The breath fogging between them was half his, half hers. For a moment he looked at her with such love that she felt lush, lost, as fragile as gold.

The illusion disappeared in a startling pool of yellow light that beamed, blindingly, on both their faces. Stix's head jerked up. He froze. So did she.

The policeman in the tall black boots with the thick gloves and long flashlight was Harvey Curtis. He had coffee at Stix's restaurant on his break every morning. His eldest kid was in "Ms. Markham's" anthro 101 class.

"Well, now." Boots buried in snow, he shoved at his cap and scratched his chin. "Seems I got a call to bring in the two teenagers screamin' down this hill louder than banshees. Figured I'd take 'em in and call their parents." A sound like a chortle rumbled from his throat before he switched off his flashlight.

"So what happened?" Kay demanded.

"Not you, too!" Susan kept her voice low, since several students at the back of the class were still gathering up their books within hearing range. "What are you doing out this early on a Monday morning? Where are the kids?"

"In preschool. I just dropped them off and stopped for a coffee at Stix's." Kay's eyes danced as she trailed Susan from the classroom. "His place is packed. Lots of jokes being passed about snowmen. Now what happened after the policeman showed up?"

"He drove us home, that's what happened. I'm sure you knew that without asking—nothing is sacred in this town. I need caffeine before I face my next class." Susan aimed for the concession machines with the speed of the driven. "You ever faced a lecture hall of a hundred kids grinning at you?"

"Not recently."

"I stopped at the bakery yesterday. All I wanted was day-old bread, but Mr. Gateway threw in a half dozen cherry doughnuts free of charge."

"Ah."

Once Kay had a cup, Susan reshifted her books, briefcase and purse, punched her coins into the slot and pushed the button for black. "Yesterday afternoon, the car needed gas. I fill it self-serve, you understand, but Jake Withers still comes out and starts rubbing my windshield. Said it was real nice Stix had finally found himself 'a nice girl.' Now I know it's a petty thing, but I absolutely hate it when people call grown women girls."

"Umm."

She retrieved the full Styrofoam cup and took a long sip. The coffee tasted like black mud and promptly burned her tongue. She savored another sip. "This morning, I passed Mr. Bridgman in the hall. He's the old, white-haired sober-faced gent who teaches philosophy. I've been trying to get a smile out of that man for the past three years. He took one look at me, said hello, and started guffawing."

"Umm?"

"Harvey told the whole damn town. How am I ever going to live this down?"

"It could be worse," Kay consoled her.

"How?"

Kay followed her into the small, empty first-floor classroom. "You could have been caught with frostbite on your tush." She murmured blandly, "Was that a possibility?"

"Of course not!"

"You've been seeing a lot of each other."

"Not like that." Susan set her briefcase and notes on the desk with a thump, which unfortunately made her coffee slosh. She licked at the hot liquid on her finger, thinking that Murphy was operating with a vengeance this morning.

She could tell from the look in Kay's eyes that her friend wasn't going to be satisfied with a running monologue of anecdotes, and unlike everyone else, Kay had the right to pry. Susan had given her that right when they'd become friends. No subject had been taboo between them. At least until now.

"Why not 'like that'?" Kay perched on the teacher's desk. "Here I'm the one who set you two up, and I have yet to hear a progress report."

"Did you hear there was a sale at Tri-State on kids clothes?" No one had used the classroom yet that day. Susan turned on the lights and started pushing chairs together. Her second class was a discussion group.

Kay crossed her legs and thoughtfully regarded her friend over the rim of her coffee cup. "It has to be pretty serious if you're not talking," she said casually, but when that didn't get a rise, she shifted gears. "He ever tell you how he was raised? His mom died when he was pretty young. His old man had a lot of money and a lot of power—timber around Coeur d'Alene—but he had definite ideas about son rearing. He wanted Stix to be a real man. You know. Ambitious and ruthless. Macho. Tough."

The look in Susan's eyes was so stricken that Kay swiftly continued. "Used to knock Stix around a little—now there's a way to toughen up a kid—and left him alone in the woods for a week one time when he was eleven. Stix wasn't supposed to come home until he'd bagged a deer. Seems he had no interest in killing things, and Stix does have a stubborn streak. By the time his father gave in and went looking for him, he was sick and suffering from exposure, had to be hospitalized—"

"Don't tell me any more, all right?" Susan stopped pushing chairs. Acid churned in her stomach for the mental pictures Kay was creating.

She felt no surprise that Stix's mother had died young, that he came from a wealthy background. Those clues clicked into place with other things she knew of him. But she'd never guessed about his father. She knew no hunters, no men who regularly needed to prove themselves with a gun and a kill. It meant nothing to her, but it would to Stix. She thought of his incredible sensitivity and patience with children, his aversion to cruelty in any form, his gentleness....

"Lot of things I only heard hearsay. I didn't really know him until we were both sixteen," Kay went on. "I was his first date. By that time, we're talking a kid who was shy to the point of agony, a kid who took it for granted he was a failure and a disappointment. We're talking a kid going crazy trying to please a father he didn't have a prayer in hell of pleasing—at least not in this life."

"Kay—"

"Just stay shut up for a minute more, Susan. I know you've got a class, and I have to go." Kay closed one eye, aimed her empty Styrofoam cup for the wastebas-

ket, tossed it and missed. Making a moue for her
klutziness, she jumped off the desk to retrieve it.

"He's been a friend for years. I adore him, but
knowing Stix—*really* knowing him—is something else.
I'm not sure anyone does. He does a lot of work with
troubled kids—you'll never hear him talk about it. And
he spends odd patches of spare time in Coeur d'Alene—
doing what, is anyone's guess. He doesn't talk. Heck,
I've never even heard him talk about a rotten cold or a
bad mood, have you?"

Susan murmured, "No."

Kay's smile was wry. "He's a man, not a boy, and
he's man enough to have made his peace with his father a long time ago. We all move past our childhood
traumas at some time, and darn it, I think he's done
well. Better than well. But he sure isn't quick to talk
about his personal feelings. I know. I've been trying to
get him to open up for years, which is exactly why I
brought this whole subject up."

Her smile died. "Mitch used to be awkward around
him. In fact, a long time ago I came darn close to box-
ing Mitch's ears one night. My husband does have a
little jealous streak, and he got this idea Stix had . . . an
attachment . . . for me. I know that rumor still occasionally wanders through town. I even know where it's
coming from. When we were teenagers, Stix did have an
attachment. But he never loved me. Not as a man loves
a woman. And I don't throw away friends because of
what other people think—neither does Mitch, *ever*—but
especially when those other people are dead wrong."

She started buttoning her coat. "I just wanted to tell
you that. I don't know why. It's just that I know Stix far
better than he thinks I do. If you're waiting for him to

tell you he loves you, well, I'm not sure he can. I'm not sure he even knows how.''

Kay gathered up her purse and gloves, then glanced at her watch. ''What do you think? Can I make that sale at Tri-State and still pick up the kids at eleven?''

When Kay finally left, Susan figured she had three minutes before the kids flooded in, blithely expecting someone to lead them in a discussion on reproductive strategies for monogamous species. Poor babies. At the moment she couldn't have led a coherent discussion on the *ABC*'s.

She leaned back against the desk and closed her eyes, a dozen disturbing thoughts tumbling in her mind.

Above and beyond everything else, Susan couldn't stop thinking that Kay had been subtly trying to tell her that she knew, all this time, about Stix's torch. It shouldn't have been a surprise. Susan had always understood why Stix had never gotten over Kay. Kay was sensitive and empathetic and loving. She was also too perceptive to miss a man's vulnerable feelings, too caring and loyal to reject a friend.

Kay, though, was adamantly positive that Stix had never really loved her.

So positive that Susan suddenly didn't know what to believe, what to think. What Kay said shouldn't have mattered. What Stix felt was the only thing that counted. But she had the odd sensation of having had the rug pulled out from under her.

The brick wall that had so easily kept her safe from a more emotional relationship suddenly didn't seem so strong, so high, so...solid. Anxiety doubled her heartbeat. Her temples started to throb. She felt an old ache and an ancient sensation of shakiness and fragility.

Everything Kay had said brought her closer to understanding who Stix was, what he wanted, and what he needed in his life. He'd been hurt. His childhood had been riddled with rejection and loss. His one launch into love had been more of the same. He was still searching for a home and a woman to come home for.

Susan had that woman pictured clearly in her mind. All he needed was someone secure in her ability to love, someone who would keep his bed hot and his heart safe. Someone who was sure she was right for him and never let him doubt that.

He didn't need so much. He asked for even less.

But that someone wasn't her. She knew it in her dread-fast heartbeat, in the old anxieties climbing up her veins. A woman could build a sense of self-worth from knowing herself to be reasonably good, competent, honorable, ethical, caring. But she also had to be honest about her flaws. From the time she was five years old, she'd had lesson on lesson about Susan Markham and love. It was a heck of a long track record. She'd never had a single win.

Students started flooding into the classroom. She straightened, smiled, picked up a conversation. But she thought, I won't hurt you, Stix. And if not hurting him meant finding the courage to break off the relationship, she would find that courage.

Seven

Susan lined up the tubes like soldiers on her bathroom counter. The baby-oil mousse was for her freshly shaven legs. The mud clay mask promised to purify and rejuvenate dry winter skin. Tugging her oldest terry-cloth robe around her, she read the directions on the third tube. The hair conditioner promised that in twenty short minutes, her hair would miraculously glow, gleam and shine.

An hour before, she'd walked into the drugstore for a simple bottle of aspirin. She still wasn't sure how or why she'd walked out with this feminine arsenal of self-improvement products—except that she had change on her mind. Changing Susan Markham. Preferably quickly. Hopefully totally.

Resolutely she opened the white tube. *Markham, you don't seriously believe any of this is going to make any difference.* But her lips firmed, and she promptly started plastering her hair with the white goo. There was always the slim chance that once purified, rejuvenated and gleaming, the new Susan would have a stronger character. White goo was no answer, but she had to start somewhere.

All day, she couldn't stop thinking how selfishly she'd involved herself with Stix, responding to her own needs instead of his. If she loved him, she loved him enough to do the right thing for him. That meant having the strength to stay away from moonlit snowy hillsides. That meant keeping her hands to herself. That meant no more kisses. And darn it, it meant becoming tough and cold-blooded, if that's what it took to keep from hurting him.

Momentarily she felt less tough than sticky, but determination was building. When her hair was fully globbed, she checked the time. Nine-0-one. Now for the clay pack, which appeared to be just what it said: mud. Thick, gritty and brown. The pack was half slathered on her nose, chin and cheeks when she thought she heard the muffled sound of knocking.

Grabbing a towel for her head, she raced for the front door. Predictably, no one was on the other side of the peephole. This late on a Monday night with a bitter-spiced wind and icy roads, no one was likely to visit but her imagination.

Closing herself back in the bathroom, she finished swabbing the mud on her forehead. The mudpack smelled like chalk. It appeared to dry unevenly and fast, causing tan streaks in the darker brown blotches. *You could scare small children and dogs without even trying, duckie. But the question is: Are you getting tough? Are you getting strong?*

She was getting confused, at least over time. It would take a computer calculator to synchronize when her face and hair were supposed to be done, and as she shook the baby-oil mousse container, she paused again. Someone was thumping somewhere. She opened the bathroom door and listened. Nothing. Zilch.

Exasperated with herself, she raised a bare leg to the counter and pushed the button on the mousse. Instantly, enough foam exploded out to cover a wall. The product generously squooshed through her hands as she rubbed it on one leg, and then she stopped for a third time, this time dead.

She was not imagining the thumping, knocking and rattling. The direction of the noise simply wasn't coming from her front door but the back. In principle, the two French doors in her bedroom were a back entrance leading to a fire-escape, but no one ever used them. The steps were unlit, unshoveled and steep. She shared the front door with the first-floor owners; anyone who knew her knew that. *That's very nice, Susan, but someone is obviously out there.*

She threw one horrified look at the mirror, then at her hands and mudpack-spotted robe. *Even you wouldn't do this to me, Murphy. Even you.* But the pounding accelerated in both rattling momentum and insistence while she rinsed her hands and hurled a towel over her head.

The pounding ceased the instant she switched on the overhead light in her bedroom. She would have muttered her short repertoire of swearwords, except that any facial movement made her face crack. The French doors had both top and bottom hinges, all of which were tight—she'd never even used them—and as she tried to pull at them, her heart started hammering.

The shadow outside the door was unmistakably male. If it was too dark to recognize him, her heart thumping had no relationship to fear. Robbers didn't knock. Door-to-door salesmen picked better hours. And she only knew one man who cast a six-foot-six shadow.

She desperately wanted to see Stix. But not now. Not until she was fixed, not until she was the new Susan— the one with courage and fortitude; the one who was strong enough to accept that she knew she was wrong for him and do the right thing about it.

The door popped free—too fast, making the towel slip from her head just as she tugged open the door. Stix was inside before she could rearrange the towel, and abruptly she gave up. Why bother covering her white-glue spiked hairstyle when hiding the rest was hopeless? One of her legs looked like something in a shaving-cream commercial. Her face was a cracked mosaic in brown.

"Hi, Suze."

Maybe she loved him, but not quite as much at that moment. If he'd ever cared for her, he could at least have had the decency to pretend not to recognize her. She threw up her hands. This was no time to be vain; this was a time to show her true character. "I could ask you what you're doing here and why on earth you used this back door and I could make about five thousand excuses for how I look—but never mind all that. If you'll give me five fast minutes to take a shower, I want to talk to you. I need to talk to you, Stix. I—"

Her voice trailed off when she saw the long-stemmed rose in his hand. There was just one, but it wasn't just a rose.

"I . . ."

It was a peach rose, a perfect, delicate, her favorite-color-peach rose. The bud was just opening and the petals were velvet-soft and fragile. As fragile and helpless as she suddenly felt.

"I . ."

He handed her the rose and then bent down. She saw snow crystals melting on his brows, glistening in his hair, caught the night's black stillness in his eyes. The mudpack never deterred him. His lips touched hers, as tender and fleeting as a whisper. He murmured, "You look beautiful, Susan." And then he was gone.

The next day, Stix was waiting for her when she climbed to her office after her last class. As she turned the corner of the stairs, he saw her blond head was bent over her purse. She was searching for something, which surprised him not at all. She muttered something most unladylike, glanced up and saw him.

From the look on her face he wondered why in hell he'd never brought a woman a rose before last night, but that answer was obvious. No other woman was Susan.

The fragile luster disappeared from her eyes all too quickly. He braced himself for rejection, and instead received the rare gift of a flustered Susan. Her cheeks flushed, her tush tightened, and her mouth made a fine barometer for her emotions. When the winds of worry were blowing, she had to work to keep those two lips steady. She was working. "Mr. Sperling!"

So. They were going to play this light and c-a-r-e-f-u-l-l-y. "Yes, ma'am?"

She unlocked her office and pointed to her desk. "Were you the one responsible for sending me that present this morning?"

He obediently ambled closer to her desk, where a white cardboard box was surrounded by stacks of papers and books. The box contained a cake—layers of chocolate, whipped cream and cherries repeated three times. The bakery called its confection Sin Cake. One full third of it was missing.

"Well? Did you do that to me, you dog?" she demanded.

"Why do I have a feeling that a wise man wouldn't answer that question?" He stuck a finger into the frosting and tested. No false advertising here. If the taste didn't tempt her toward sin, nothing would.

Hard as she tried, her voice softened. "I loved the rose, Stix. That was a lovely thing to do."

"You liked the cake best, from the look of what's missing."

"I had two pieces of cake this morning and immediately called Weight Watchers. Not to enroll. To give them your name. I hate to give advice but if I were you, I'd leave town. What they do to people like you is so unpleasant that I can't even discuss it in mixed company."

"Am I mixed company?"

"You're worse, and now stop this! Stix, I have to tell you something."

He figured that was coming, which was why he'd already thrown himself on the carved-back wooden chair and stretched out his legs. Blows were easier to take when a man was relaxed.

"Actually, I want to talk to you about two things, but this just won't wait." In a giant rush, she blurted out, "In my opinion, real men cook. Real men also love rocking a baby. I know people our age were all raised with the Marlboro man as an ideal, but I never bought him. You can't measure integrity and self-respect by the size of a man's biceps. And a really strong man doesn't have to carry a club.''

Coming out of the total blue, the context of her practiced little speech startled and moved him. His throat felt suddenly thick. He had to clear it before he could talk. "By any chance," he asked her gently, "has anyone been recently telling you tales about my father?''

"Your father? I don't know your father from Adam. This has nothing to do with you personally. I just wanted to tell you—''

"Yes, I heard you." He admired a woman who could lie with a straight face. "And now I have something to tell you.''

"What?'' She looked as wary as a cornered fawn.

"That brown face gunk worked. You're so gorgeous you take my breath away and Shakespeare would screw up a sonnet doing justice to your fantastic hair. But, Susan?'' He only thought she was tense. He saw her lips start to twitch into a grin.

"What?''

"I'll be darned if I can figure out what you were trying to do to your legs.''

"Cream them.''

"Like butter and sugar in a cake mix?'' He leaned over the chair so he had a better view of her legs. "They whipped up in fine shape," he said blandly.

"Was that a compliment? It was wrapped in such a sick pun that I couldn't tell.''

"You liked it," he informed her.

But that was the problem. She liked everything he did, and this entire conversation was getting away from her. "Could we get serious here, shorty?''

"That's what I came for: to deliver a serious invitation. We need to skip town, Suze, and I have an ideal place for it. This weekend. The family has a cabin on the back side of Coeur d'Alene. Ten-foot fireplace and a loft. Four beds—count 'em four—meaning that there are limitless potentials for both orgies and celibacy. Not that you don't trust me. I know you do. So, more relevant: do you have a pair of cross-country skis?"

As he stood he saw her brows arch in bewilderment. "Wait a minute! What is this about needing to skip town? And I'm not sure how a weekend or cross-country skis got into this conversation."

"Don't tell me you haven't taken the heat for two days about our little midnight snow junket? If we stick around, the whole town's going to marry us off, and you don't want that. If we stay out of sight for a couple of days, the gossips will move on to fresh prey."

"I've heard creative excuses for a weekend off in my time, but that one's beyond shaky."

He thought it was pretty good. It was certainly distracting her from the original serious talk she'd had in mind. "How long has it been since you've had a couple of honestly free days?" he continued blandly. "Face it, Suze, you've been a little nervous lately. Look how tense you were when Harvey nearly arrested us for disturbing the peace on Saturday night, and the rose didn't seem to help." He paused. "You do know why I gave you the rose, don't you?"

"Because of my nerves?" she asked dryly. His steady stream of nonsense was exhausting her.

"No. Do you want a second guess?"

He was teasing, but suddenly she wasn't. She clutched her arms under her chest and met his eyes with honest vulnerability. "Stix, we need to talk about that, because no. I honestly have no idea why you gave me that rose,'' she said quietly.

All he could think of was that for all her sass and flaunty confidence, her quick mind and competence, Susan wouldn't have any idea why a man would send her roses.

Susan was smart about everything but Susan. She gave him absolutely no choice but to haul her close. He did, with a swiftness she couldn't anticipate. He laid a kiss on her mouth with enough pressure to shock her, stole her tongue the instant her lips parted, and slid his hands deliberately, intimately, down her spine to her bottom.

If it had been anyone else but Susan, he would have felt foolish pulling off such cavalier aggressiveness. Valentino-like dramatics were for other men. He hadn't miraculously changed into some other man, but this was different. This was necessary.

He'd given her a rose because she deserved roses. She also deserved diamonds and violets and furs, and a man who could kiss her the way she should be kissed: thoroughly, passionately, abandon-the-rules fiercely.

He knew exactly how he wanted her kissed. The trick was doing it, but his clear-cut motivations blurred somewhere between the scent of her perfume and the feel of her body heating under his hands. Good intentions dissolved when he felt her small breasts tighten, her hands climb his shoulders. And a moment's brash impulse became enormously complicated because Susan yielded more every time he kissed her. But she didn't want to.

He wanted her to want to.

When he lifted his head, her eyes had a dazed glow and her lips were crushed coral. There was something in the way she looked that irrevocably changed who he thought he was as a man—and who he wanted and needed to be as a man.

He slowly released her, savoring that look in her eyes, aware she was fighting as hard to gain control as she'd fought for anything. To make that easier for her, he chose a light tone he knew she could deal with. "I know that was out of line, but it keeps occurring to me that there are probably a lot of men out there who've fed you the line about appreciating your mind. With me, it's strictly the body, Suze. I just wanted you to know I never gave a hoot in hell about your gray matter."

"Stix?"

"Hmm?" She said his name as breathily as if she were talking long-distance from Paris. He loved it.

"You like my mind."

"Not compared with your legs," he firmly corrected her. "Anyone ever tell you how much you love being kissed?"

"Shorty, you're disruptive and upsetting. Are you leaving soon?"

"Are you going with me on Friday?"

"I have too much work."

"So bring it."

"You have a restaurant at its busiest on a weekend."

"That's going to be Sal's problem." He loped toward the door. "So... pick you up at five o'clock on Friday night and don't forget your long johns." He was gone, gently closing the door behind him.

He was becoming good at fast exits, she thought fleetingly. He was under the mistaken impression that he eluded an argument if he escaped in time. He hadn't eluded anything. All she had to do was open the door and shout a good loud "No." Any twenty-nine-year-old woman could say no and make it stick—when she wanted to.

Susan sank into the desk chair and pushed two fingers to her temples. The wisest word in the English language was *no*, so why did she have such a hard time with it where Stix was concerned?

But she knew why, just as she knew that a rose and a baker's sinful offering changed nothing. She wasn't going to be his lover. She wasn't going to be the woman to make him forget Kay. But she loved that man more than rainbows. A man reaching out for love for the first time in years didn't need a rejection in the form of a cold-blooded "No." She just couldn't do that to him. Maybe a quiet weekend away would make an honest talk easier.

If she were unwilling to be a lover, she simply couldn't be less than a friend.

"Just your average old rustic cottage, hmm?" Susan had taken the ninety-mile trek to Coeur d'Alene before, sometimes just for the drive. The road crossed swirling rivers, passed deep ravines, and climbed and curled over roller-coaster hills before ending at the lake. Tonight, though, a driving rain had obliterated most of the view, and as she stepped out of the car, she was promptly soaked.

It supposedly never rained in northern Idaho in December, but there was no arguing with the sky. The out-of-season downpour was relentlessly turning white fluff to slush and crystal-snow prettiness to lead gray. She barely noticed. She hadn't stopped staring at Stix since they'd passed through a ten-foot wrought-iron gate a half mile back on the deserted road. Now, hands on hips, she couldn't stop staring at his family "cabin."

Choice homes were sprinkled all over Coeur d'Alene, but not all lake lovers were millionaires. Her image of a cabin was four log walls and a bunk bed, and her choice of old jeans and ancient red sweatshirt reflected their presumed destination. She saw no log walls, but the rough stone and tall Gothic arches of a dark, sprawling miniature castle. Clustered in a tall green glen of pines, the elegant sentinel perched on a ravine over-looking a private cove of the lake. Mullioned windows glinted black in the night gloom. The double doors were of carved oak, with a brass lion for a door knocker.

Stix had been extraordinarily quiet on the drive up. Now she knew why. She stalked back to the trunk, where he was piling gear into his arms. "You slightly misled me, shorty," she said politely.

He glanced up, but only long enough to notice her empty arms. He handed her a duffel bag and box. "You were expecting outside plumbing?"

"I was expecting anything but this!"

"Good, that was the idea." He shot her a grin. "But don't get your hopes too high. The inside may be in nip-and-tuck shape. No one's spent any time in the place for the last ten years except an old man who does a weekly stint as a caretaker."

"No one's been in the place? But I thought you said it was the family cabin." She carefully enunciated the word "cabin."

"It was my father's getaway place for a long time, until he handed me the deed for it when I was twenty-one. I've never had the time to fool with it till now. Come on, let's get you in and out of the rain." In short order he had the door unlocked, a light switched on and an armful of gear dropped right inside. "Explore. I'll bring in the rest of the stuff from the car."

He pushed up his collar and hustled back into the rain. She nearly followed him. She could hardly let him get away with dropping little bombs like this without explanation. The last thing she knew, Stix didn't have a life-style involving caretakers, choice bits of property in Coeur d'Alene, and mullion-windowed abodes deserted for the past decade.

She hesitated in the doorway for a long moment, and then abruptly shed her wet boots and jacket. Expecting direct answers out of Talkative Charlie was like finding volunteers for a root canal. Something had been on Stix's mind for the entire drive up, and her best coax-and-tease humor hadn't budged his oddly pensive mood.

Alone now, she shivered and wrapped her arms under her chest. She'd had a thousand reservations about coming this weekend, but never as many as when she'd seen the exterior of this place. Now she felt an increasing tense, off-balance mood as she started exploring.

Within three steps, she formed a fierce, fast, and blindly emotional dislike for Stix's father. It wasn't the place. The terrazzo-tiled hall led into a massive and comfortable living room. She switched on lights, noting the ten-foot-high stone fireplace, the elegant arched ceiling, the forest-green overstuffed couches and chairs, the gleam of a mahogany gaming table. If that were all that was to the room, she would have loved it, but there was more.

The values of Stix's father were as clear as a soup-can label, and totally at odds with everything she knew of Stix. A wet bar sat in the far corner, stocked well and thoroughly with expensive brands of hard liquor. The furniture centered around a huge white polar-bear rug—a real one—and she couldn't turn around without find-

ing other animals "staring" at her. A moose head hung
from one wall, an elk and antlered deer from another.
A collection of rifles shone from behind the glass of a
locked cabinet.

The walls that could have made a sheltering haven
were of cold stone. Above, a lanai stretched the width
of the living room. The loft appeared to be the master
bedroom; open, so that even upstairs there would be no
escaping the view of all those dead trophies.

A kitchen and dining area adjoined the main living
room. She found a luxurious grill, a brick fireplace large
enough to roast a boar, and a trestle table designed to
feed twenty. The first floor also had a bath, complete
with an ebony sunken tub and a mirrored wall. The
fixtures were brass lion heads. A bear's head hung over
the sink

She stared for a long time at the sad-looking grizzly,
then searched out the source of clutter and thuds ema-
nating from the kitchen. Still wearing his jacket, Stix
was unpacking food supplies from a cardboard box.
Except for a damp head, he didn't look any different
than he always looked—tall, blue-jeaned, sexy as sin
and incorrigibly easy. She was the one who couldn't
seem to feel easy. Something about the whole place
made her hurt, as if she'd like to karate-chop a brick
wall or throw something hard.

Instead, she lifted bread and milk from the box—or
started to. Stix had the box whisked out of her sight and
carted to the far counter before she could blink, but not
before she noticed the rest of its contents. "That one's
full of heavy stuff," he told her. "I'll do it."

"Fine." She asked casually, "Spend much time here
growing up?"

"Some."

"I had no idea Hemingway was alive and well in Coeur d'Alene." She added, "I don't want to be indelicate, but there's no chance I can go to the bathroom with that bear staring at me."

His eyes glinted amusement. "My father would be disappointed you didn't like his Alaskan grizzly."

"I'd like to meet your father. Maybe five or six hundred years from now, when I'm in a nice, kind, objective mood." The comment slipped out before she could stop it.

Stix handed her a grocery sack, filled, she noticed, with totally innocuous items. He also looked at her for a split second. "Most women like him on sight, Suze. Don't assume you wouldn't."

"If and when I meet him, I'll be polite. I won't embarrass you. Just keep me away from sharp objects and we'll probably get along just fine." Another spilled-milk comment that she hadn't meant to make. Hurriedly she ducked her head and applied intense concentration to a roll of paper towels. The cupboard closest to the sink had a wooden towel roller. She nearly had the handle unscrewed when she felt Stix's palm cup her nape.

"Susan..." For a minute his fingers kneaded and caressed, then skated down her back and dropped. "The lake's special in winter, so are the woods, and so can this place be when a fire's roaring in the living room, which I'll get to. I wanted you to see this place for lots of reasons, but none of them had anything to do with my father. Since he seems to have popped into this conversation, though, I don't know who told you what, but gossip's never the whole story."

"So tell me what I should know." Still not looking at him, she finished putting the towel on the roller.

"Nothing is ever black-and-white. Something twisted in my father when my mother died." His tone stayed simple and quiet. "I'm not saying he wasn't a first-class bastard when I was growing up. Just that it's all done now. It was all done a long time ago."

She turned then. "If it were all done, you would have been living in this house."

He shook his head. "There was never any chance of my doing that. My father gave me this place in apology...for a lot of things. If I'd lived in it, it would have been the same as letting him think he could right all wrongs with gifts of money or property, and that's a mistake my father's made too much in his life. When he started trying again, though, so did I. We don't see eye-to-eye about much of anything, but we have a relationship of a kind, which is more than we used to. He's alone and he's always going to be alone, and there's no holding a grudge against a man that unhappy, Suze. Put your claws back in. He's not my enemy."

"He hurt you," she said fiercely.

A ghost of a smile. "Honey, there's just no point in kicking a man who's already down."

She wanted to let it go and couldn't. "You feel that way because you're a good man, a decent man. I'm a more rotten breed of woman, Stix. I could easily kick him and not look back."

Again he shook his head, this time leaning back against the counter, unpacking forgotten. His eyes drifted over her face, warm as only Stix's eyes could be, but oddly immutable, enigmatic. "I love the loyal lioness, but to arouse your protective instincts was never why I brought you here. Among other reasons, I wanted to warn you. The legacy's more than a house deed and some childhood memories. At some point you had to

know that. My father has a small fortune in a lumbering business, for which I was trained to take over from
the time I was in diapers. He'll retire in three years.''

She froze, a package of paper plates in her hand.

''I take an active role on the board now, just not in
direct management. I figure I'll deal with other choices
when it's time and when I have to, but it was only fair
to warn you. Security is nice, but I don't envision an
upgrade to Mercedes in my life-style. I like a Jeep and I
like jeans, and the restaurant is mine. I've worked for
it and I value it. There may come a point when I give it
up, but I'll never be the kind to get into double mar-
tinis before dinner.''

''No?''

''No.''

''You don't think a diamond pinkie ring would suit
you?''

''Nope.''

''No stress ulcers, no barbecues with your banker, no
designer suits?''

''Sorry, Suze.''

She dropped the paper plates on the counter and slid
her hands around his neck. Her gesture appeared to
startle him. It startled her, too.

She'd had every intention of keeping her hands off
him this weekend, but he was the one making that impossible. All his little surprises had her head reeling,
starting with the money implicit in this place and ending with the compassion he felt for his father. Suddenly it was too easy to see her Stix of the ragged
sweatshirt managing in a boardroom, and it shook her
thoroughly when he'd started talking about the future
as if she had a right to know. None of those were the
reasons she stood on tiptoe. Stix was missing a smile, his

eyes were too serious and his shoulders too taut. She rose up to kiss his mouth, no-nonsense quickly and no-nonsense hard. "As if I could give a hoot. Don't you ever say 'Sorry, Suze' to me again," she told him severely.

"Sorry, Suze."

She kissed him again.

"Sorry, Suze. Sorry, Suze. Sorry, Suze."

The devil puckered his lips, waiting, the dance back in his eyes, and she knew their serious talk was all done. She eased back down on the balls of her feet and gave him a little push. "You're a wicked, greedy man. You're also sneaky."

"Sneaky?"

"You think I didn't see the two bottles of champagne wrapped in the bottom of the box? I thought we came up here to ski."

"We can't ski in the rain."

Her eyes searched his, although she was still smiling. "Did you pack the champagne before or after you knew the weatherman predicted rain?"

"Before. I bought the champagne last Tuesday."

"And what else did you preplan, shorty?"

"A wild orgy, breakfast in bed tomorrow morning, champagne served in the bath..."

He gave a long list of lascivious plans until she started laughing, but that laughter was really to please him, to reassure him that she wasn't taking him seriously.

On the inside, adrenaline was suddenly, inexplicably, pumping through her blood. A ghostly wind howled through the cracks in the windows, and she suddenly shivered.

Eight

Stix saw her shiver. He nearly gave a roar of pure masculine satisfaction, but he didn't have time. Impatience, purpose, and vitality had his blood pumping faster than a horse's at the racetrack. He had to move if his plans for the evening were ever going to work. "About time I got you fed before you starve. How good are you at shredding lettuce?"

"It's one of my finer culinary talents," Susan assured him.

"Can you make a salad dressing?"

"You mean can I pour from a bottle?"

"No!" He promptly forbade her to go anywhere near anything except the head of lettuce, and then regretfully had to ignore her. He had a thousand things to do, and all of them immediately.

The first priority was to miraculously get the champagne chilled in the hour before dinner. A wine connoisseur might not have approved his popping the two bottles temporarily into the freezer, but necessity made it a must. After that, he started his chicken, then hauled in wood from the stacked bin in the backyard.

It took a good fifteen minutes to get a healthy blaze going in the living-room fireplace, then it was back to the kitchen. While his chicken was crisping, he concentrated on the "vin" part of the "coq au vin" recipe, whistling a college fight song under his breath. The schedule was tight but everything was going fine—better than fine.

After setting the chicken in the oven, he cleaned the broccoli, added basil and thyme to the pot, and began to blend the cheese sauce. When that was all started, he flicked the switch on the chandelier over the trestle table and ducked underneath for his hidden cache of supplies. Setting the table was next: two Lenox dinner plates, two crystal flute glasses, his mother's sterling candlesticks, and two red Irish-linen mats. The lady in the store said he had to have mats, and Suze liked red. Somewhere he'd packed two candles.

"Ah...shorty?"

He was jogging back to the stove and swung an arm around Suze's neck. A fast squeeze was all he had time for. She was so busy staring at the table she barely noticed. "All done shredding your lettuce?" he asked cheerfully.

"What is all this? What happened to the paper plates?"

"You'll see." At least, he hoped she saw.

Days before, he'd racked his brain for anything more romantic and imaginative than the old champagne/candlelight/bear-rug-by-the-fire routine. Coming up with more exotic ideas had been easy. It had taken him a little longer to understand that exotic wasn't at all what he wanted. Susan could ignore subtlety. She couldn't possibly misunderstand the old standards, and rather than trying to hide what he was doing, he wanted to shout it. This is not an accident, Suze. Make no mistake. It is specifically and deliberately for you.

Besides—not that she needed to know—he'd never even tried to pull off champagne and candlelight before. First-time sledders didn't audition with the luge. At the moment he was slightly frantic just trying to master the basics.

He found a spare four minutes to tug off his sweatshirt and change into a tie and white shirt—starched, good linen, one of Susan's picks. That was when the avalanche started.

The problems started out small enough. When he returned to the kitchen after changing his shirt, he found his candles, only they wobbled in the holders because he'd bought the wrong size. Lit, wobbly candles were unsafe. They also looked stupid. He could handle basic engine repairs, but the candles just weren't going to stand up straight. And then Susan appeared at his side.

"Umm, Stix? We have a slight excess of smoke in the living room."

Susan's "slight excess" was a fast-billowing, eye-burning smoke cloud. Right off, he guessed no real danger existed—the chimney was simply damp from so many years of nonuse—but obviously the whole fireplace system had to be checked to make sure. Opened doors and a damper adjustment ultimately solved the problem, but the total checkout took time.

In the meantime, his chicken had burned and he found Susan trying to save the cheese sauce for his broccoli. She took one quick look at his face, and her tone rolled out like soothing water: "Now just take it easy. Everything's fine. I love things well-done!"

He was not soothed. The candles still wouldn't fit, and by then his shirt had a soot smudge and was all untucked and messy. Worse than that, he'd forgotten the champagne. Frozen champagne expanded. Both bottles had popped their corks in the freezer. The resultant mess was a horror. He found a mop. She found a rag. The cheese sauce turned crispy.

The finished menu included dried, burned chicken, beer in the flute glasses, and limp broccoli. The overhead light provided as much atmosphere as the scent of burned cheese sauce. Susan never took her eyes off him. She also ate everything on her plate and asked for seconds. He could have killed her.

He insisted on doing the dishes alone, mostly so he could lick his wounds in peace. That didn't work. The window over the sink overlooked a change in the weather. It was dead black outside, but the rain had turned into a driving sleet storm. The one thing he'd been sure of this weekend was snow. His plans for the next day included skiing and exploring the countryside with Susan. Both options withered in front of his eyes. The wind howled like a frustrated banshee.

He was too exhausted to howl himself, but he wouldn't have minded assuming a six-foot-six fetal position someplace where he wouldn't have to face Susan when she came out of the bathroom. That was when the fuse blew.

"I can fix a fuse!" Susan yelled out from behind the closed bathroom door. "Don't get upset! This is nothing! Markham may not be too swift at salad dressings, but she knows her fifteen- and thirty-amp fuses!"

She did know her fifteen- and thirty-amp fuses. Actually, so did he, but she found the one with the burned wire first, and there died his last chance to play hero. "Now—" Susan herded him out of the utility room with her vibrantly cheerful tone on loud "—I saw some cognac behind that wet bar. I'll get us both a snifter and then we're going to relax in front of that fantastic fire you built. Aren't you beat? What a long day!"

She sipped her cognac like a lady; he gulped his like a dose of medicine. When she took both glasses to the kitchen, he crashed flat, prone and tense on the polar-bear rug. The instant she came back in, he planned to say something funny and light—as soon as he could think of it. For the moment he closed his eyes and didn't exactly feel low; more like destroyed.

The dinner...was just a dinner. And Susan had a great sense of humor. So did he. But he'd never felt quite so conscious of not being an exciting Redford, a wicked Gable, a devilish Newman.

He'd survived those lacks in his character before and never missed them. But Susan must miss them. She never made much of her background but he had a clear enough picture. She'd grown up among strangers, with no one to share the loss of her parents, no one she could count on. Then along came her Karn. He knew Suze had him labeled a real nice guy. Stix had him labeled below seaweed. The guy couldn't handle his own problems so he'd piled them all on her, then wrapped her up tightly with guilt and blame.

No one had it easy, and Suze had had it tougher than most. Yet she'd pulled herself up and made something special of her life. He was proud of her. He respected her. And it had been slowly killing him that Suze had never had anyone to fuss or spoil her.

He was only a man, but for one evening he'd wanted to be more. He'd hoped to come off as daring, sure, bold—and heck, a little stud thrown into the image wouldn't have hurt. He'd just wanted to give Susan something she didn't have. He'd wanted her to feel desired. He'd wanted her to feel spoiled. He'd wanted her to feel valued.

Instead, he'd flopped flatter than a pancake. Five, six hundred years from now, he would undoubtedly find it funny. But not tonight.

When he felt movement next to him, he opened his eyes, and found a firelit silhouette playing tricks on his mind. A few sips of cognac hardly justified hallucinations. "What are you doing?"

"Pulling off my sweater. What does it look like I'm doing? It's hot by the fire."

He knew that. They'd turned out all the light switches when the fuse blew, and hadn't turned them back on because they were unnecessary. The flames licking around the giant fireplace logs provided a bright yellow glow of light and also heat. Neither explained Susan's actions. "Suze?" he murmured tactfully.

"Hmm?"

"You aren't wearing anything under that sweater."

She glanced down. "True." She smiled. "*Heavens*, it's warm."

She meant the room. He forgot the room. She was built small. Her breasts were ivory with dark chocolate tips. Tiny tips. The nipples had a sassy tilt, like the woman, and they were tight and hard—probably from nervousness. Susan was liberated, but not *this* liberated.

He watched her pull off one sock, then the other, then rise to a kneeling position where it was easier for her to unbutton and unzip her jeans. She smiled at him as she pushed those off, and gathering up her clothes, stood up.

She used her jeans to cover the moose head, and then moved to the elk. After blocking the elk's eyes with her socks, she crossed the room to the antlered buck. She skimmed her hands into the waistband of her underpants. Down they went and then up, to make blinders for the deer.

He considered telling her that a quarter ounce of transparent pink hardly blocked a twelve-point buck, but when a man's heart is in his throat, talking was tricky. Stuffed deer were difficult to keep on his mind. She came to her own conclusions anyway, retrieved her sweater from where she'd tossed it, and draped it over the deer horns.

The only voyeur left in the room was himself. His blood raced as she moved toward him, bare as a wood nymph but dangerously more seductive. Her hair picked up the light of the flames when she knelt down. Her skin glowed, and when she leaned over him, her eyelashes looked thick and dusty, like black velvet on cream. The look of her mouth made him forget to breathe. He didn't need air, anyway.

"Suze?"

"Hmm?"

"I'm not complaining, you understand, but did something happen this evening that I don't know about? See, last thing I knew the champagne froze. The chicken burned. The candles—"

"Wobbled. Yes. I was there."

"I just wanted to be sure you weren't confused."

"I'm not confused," she murmured.

"Because if I had any idea you responded this way to burned chicken, I would have burned chicken two months ago. Hell, I would have bought an entire chicken farm and—"

"You're talking an awful lot," she admonished him. "I'm the one who talks when they're nervous, remember?"

"I'm just not . . . sure . . . what you're doing."

"At the moment, I'm washing your ear. With my tongue. And biting the lobe. With my teeth. And you must like it, Mr. Sperling, because your body temperature just went up forty degrees." She lifted her head and whispered demurely, "Let's move on to what else you like. Or do you need that tie?"

He made a very odd sound. Susan took it to mean a no, he didn't need the tie, and slowly loosened the knot. His shirt had five buttons. She took care of those, too, aware he was staring at her more cautiously than a lit stick of dynamite. She didn't exactly have a history of being sexually aggressive. He wasn't objecting—his eyes were as black as night and bright as fire—but he was definitely expecting a catch.

There wasn't one, and to prove that she trailed her lips over the taut slope of his shoulders, licked a meandering trail along the line of his collarbone, and kissed his Adam's apple. His skin was bronze by firelight, streaked with light and shadow.

His breath turned rampant, hers catchy. Somewhere, sleet pelted against the windows and the shadow of flames flickered on the walls.

He hadn't moved to touch her yet, but that was fine. It was his response she wanted to kindle, not her own, and she didn't have to go far to find flame. When she skidded a palm down his thigh, his heart slammed.

When she planted kisses between the springy hairs on his chest, every muscle in his body hardened and tensed. When her hand drifted near the zipper of his jeans, his eyes took on the heat and spit of fire.

A roar of fear in her ears made her hesitate. She banished it. She already knew all the reasons this was wrong, and all the reasons it was right. His lips tasted like cognac and fire, like searching and loneliness and need. He tasted like a man who needed to be made love to, and it was totally his fault that she was doing this. She'd seen how he was after dinner. Crushed. He actually thought she cared about his burned chicken.

No woman alive cared about burned chicken. A man who exposed himself to risk, who reached out with vulnerability and caring—those were the ingredients that tore a woman apart.

She swept a fierce line of kisses up his chest, around his neck, across his jaw. Maybe she'd sworn not to hurt him, but there was no way on earth she could not love him. She knew what he wanted. This night, the gift was free, and her hands became more reckless, her kisses bolder.

Fear rushed at her again, louder this time, a jangle of dissonance where she wanted none. Temptation was the texture of his skin; touching him with honesty and openness was a heady pleasure. She was acutely, vibrantly aware of all five senses—it was just the sixth sense that made her hands tremble. *I don't care whose name you call out, Stix. I swear I don't. I love you. It's just . . . a little harder to risk than I thought.*

In one smooth motion, she found herself abruptly shifted to her back and pinned. Stix snuggled a blue-jeaned leg intimately between hers, and he captured both her busy hands. His long taut body was ample proof of total and urgent sexual arousal, but that's not what she saw in his eyes. Her palms dampened for the dominant possessiveness she saw in his features, the liquid intent in his gaze. "Did you think I wouldn't notice?" he scolded softly.

"'Notice'?"

"Suze, you're coming on to me faster than a forest fire, and you're delicious in passion. You're delicious when you lose your head. You're even delicious when you're so tense you can't breathe."

"I'm not tense—"

"You won't be," he agreed, then whispered, "You're not afraid of anything that could happen, not with me—but if you don't know that, you will."

He never gave her a chance to answer, he simply drank from her mouth as deeply as he would have drunk from a long, dark well. Her lips yielded, then her tongue. Still, he saw that crushing vulnerability shimmering in her eyes, and he moved down to lace a string of kisses around her throat. He knew she liked that string because her fingers climbed up his arms and dug into his shoulders.

He shifted down to where the firelight streaked color on her soft breasts. Dark excitement shot through her for the first lash of his tongue, and his tongue was warm, wet, relentless. She arched toward him, as if under the naive impression that her willingness was all he wanted.

Instinct drove him, not reason. Emotion, not sense, ruled his actions. Earlier in the evening, he'd wanted to be a Gable or a Redford for her. Not now. To hell with the heroes. They didn't know Susan. *He* did. She knew little of her own pleasures, he'd discovered that before, but he hadn't known that she had some association with making love and being hurt.

He imbedded kisses first on the butter-soft skin on her abdomen, then on the intimate crease of her inner thigh. He made her jump when he nipped. He made her smile when he kissed all ten of her toes.

She was no longer smiling when his palm cupped the soft, warm nest between her thighs. She bucked toward him blindly, and her eyes closed when his mouth fused on hers again. He wanted her pleasure and he wanted it now, and he showed her in that kiss. He showed her with the dip and stroke of his fingers and palm, and suddenly she was holding on for dear life.

So was he. Her first soft, explosive cry turned his heart to flammable liquid. She was his. She was life. She was a need that had never had a name until he knew her. Her eyes were all blurred from that first burst of pleasure, her skin all hot, her lips all trembly. She wasn't expecting more.

He'd given her nothing yet. Passion had more facets than a diamond. Long before this night was over, he had in mind knowing Susan as only a man who loves a woman can know her.

The fire roared when a log fell. Susan heard it, and she felt the scratchy roughness of the bear rug beneath her spine. Both were distracting calls of reality. Neither distracted her from a drowning sensation of fragility. She could break. He seemed to know that. He seemed to want that.

He wasn't her gentle, tender Stix at all but a demanding stranger, an alluring, dangerous lover who had no respect for limits and boundaries. He sought her pleasure, courted it, wooed it, and when he heard her shameless cry he did the unforgivable: he called her name—*her* name. Over and over and over....

Breathless, she closed her eyes for a long moment, caught up in weakness and wonder. She was supremely conscious that the man busy wreathing kisses all over her face had taken nothing for himself yet. He'd just shattered her. She'd expected to freeze up. He hadn't let that happen. She'd expected to bog down on issues of inadequacy and ghosts. Stix had left her no doubt about whom he was making love to, that there were only two people in this room, that he understood making love was a celebration.

He made the mistake of trying to shift away from her. She held him hard.

He only smiled, and loosened her hands so he could pull away. His jeans ended up in a puddle by the hearth, but before he crouched back down he closed her fingers around a bit of foil from his pocket.

Then he was back, sliding next to her, length to length. His fingers splayed in her hair and he held her face still for kiss after kiss. Bare against bare trembled through her. He'd given her a taste of wonder. Now she wanted it all, and he was long and gold and wild and male by firelight.

"Now, love," he whispered urgently.

Since he'd given her the foil, she knew what he wanted her to do, but she'd never put a condom on a man. It had never occurred to her that such a moment of responsible sanity could be unspeakably erotic. It had never occurred to her that her involvement was the same as a shout of a shared yes; that she wanted him, that she wanted this.

And she was thoroughly, wickedly fascinated by his response to her rolling the thin sheath over his man-

hood. How could she not linger? He'd nipped her behind, which was where she'd gotten the extraordinary
idea that play was part of intimacy. In her own good
time, she tried the tease of her fingertips, a butterfly of
a caress, the barest touch of her tongue...

And rather swiftly found herself flat on her back, a
large man with extraordinarily tortured eyes looming
over her. "You can play all you want," he whispered,
"tomorrow."

"You invited me to play."

"I didn't know you were going to take that as an invitation to drive me out of my mind. Now it's my turn
to love you out of your mind. Say yes, Suze. Say it loud
and clear. And honey?"

"Hmm?"

"Do me a favor and say it in one hell of a hurry."

She said, fiercely, "Yes."

At the first touch of him parting her flesh, a sound
tore from her throat and her spine arched like a drawn
bow. He drew her legs around him and whispered soft
things, wild things, and then he moved and she was lost.
He stroked her hot damp skin and wooed her to mad-
ness and rhythm with kisses and whispers and textures
and heat. He took her on a pagan ride on a streak of
lightning.

All she really knew was that with Stix, her whole body
became a heart. He was the beat. Nothing in her life had
been this natural, this right, and when that first pulse of
ecstasy took her, she could have sworn she touched the
sun. There was another and another before she felt a
wild shudder rack through him.

She was still breathless, still trembling, still silk from
the inside out when he rained a dozen kisses on her face.

"I love you, Susan." More kisses. "Love you. Love you. Love you...."

"You have to stop looking at me, shorty."

"Why?"

"Because it's two in the morning. Because you should be thinking about finding a bed to sleep in. Because you've seen it all before—and if you don't get your hands off the cookie jar, you're going to get us both in trouble for the third time."

He shifted. "So we'll talk. Let's discuss your fanny." He leaned back so he could see her face. "Have you ever had a hickey on your fanny?"

"Did anyone ever tell you that you'd make a headline failure as a monk?" Susan lurched to her feet. "I know what I'm going to do with you. Food will keep you out of trouble, and don't tell me you're not hungry. It's been hours. You're probably weak."

He was "weak" worth three roast beefs on rye, a half dozen blueberry muffins, two apples, a bottle of beer, and potato chips. The food didn't keep him out of trouble, though. He sprawled next to her on the bear rug like a sultan and regularly tempted her with bites and sips and nibbles—some even related to food.

She kept waiting for the spell to break. Making love did not eliminate gravity. The entire world had not changed. She had to get sensible and rational extremely soon, but Stix wasn't helping.

She couldn't doubt his pleasure, his satisfaction, his tenderness. He looked at her as if she were diamonds, as if he'd meant those words of love. He couldn't stop touching her. He showed no signs of ever going to sleep. He showed no signs of ever letting her out of his sight.

And for the immediate present, he offered her more temptation than she could handle.

"No," she said firmly.

"You love blueberry muffins."

"Have you absolutely no respect for a woman's body?"

"Oh, Lord. Not *another* trick question," he drawled, which made her laugh.

She fed him potato chips to make him behave, but when a crumb fell on her breast he pounced. Then she had to stretch, a languid kitten stretch that came from feeling warm and secure and crazy-happy. He claimed to find another potato-chip crumb in her navel, when there clearly wasn't one. He insisted someone had to lick the salt off her fingers, and by the time he finished that, she was lying half on top of him and getting serious.

Her tongue flicked a crumb from his lower lip, and she experimented with a tickling butterfly kiss and the sweep of her lashes on his cheek. But the quieter mood kept building inside her. Possessively she pushed back the flop of hair that always fell on his brow and found herself looking at him. *Really* looking at him.

She loved him so much. But honestly admiring him was like extra frosting; Stix was so much more than the man people first met. He'd made his own way, ignored his silver-spoon background and taken his own fork in the road. Neither wealth nor connections impressed him. He'd used no one to get where he wanted to go. He was strong and stubborn and a man of integrity. She could picture him thriving on white-water rapids. She could picture him managing his father's lumbering business. She could picture him with children—a dozen, and they'd all be devils.

She could *not* picture him out of her life, although she was doing her best to remember her common sense. It wasn't that she wanted to break the spell, but the waiting was driving her to distraction. It was knowing the roof was going to cave in but not knowing when. Twenty-nine years of bad experiences didn't erase in a few hours' time, and she would be crazy to believe they did.

Stix saw the fire in her eyes dim. One minute she was playing sprawling, teasing vamp—Lord, he loved her that way—and the next she'd tucked her face in against his shoulder. His arms tightened around her and he closed his eyes. "I meant what I said, you know."

"I don't remember what you last said, but it was undoubtedly about food. If you tempt me with one more thing, shorty—"

"I meant what I said about loving you." He felt her body brace as if he'd just delivered a blow. "You don't believe me?"

"I believe you're feeling good right now, so good you want to share it. Making love with you was the most special thing that's ever happened to me," she admitted softly. "But that doesn't mean—"

"I never told Kay that I loved her. I never told any other woman that I loved her." He rearranged her, since she was determined to lock as tense as a poker. He tucked one of her legs around his, pulled her arm back around him, and talked slow and careful and easy. "This strikes me as possibly the most tactless, insensitive, awkward time on earth to bring up another woman, Suze. But if I don't tell you how I felt about Kay, I'm afraid you'll never believe how I feel about you. Would you at least listen?"

He wished she'd smile. She touched his cheek instead, and he nuzzled his lips into the hollow of her palm. "There was never any question in my mind that I once loved Kay, but I never told her that I did. Some fancy psychologist could probably give you reasons for that. I took on a pretty good load of rejection as a kid, and built up a definite aversion to being slapped in the face. As long as I never told her how I felt, I never had to face a rejection. As long as she never knew, no one got hurt. No one was put on the line. There was nothing to spoil the picture I had in my head of an ideal love, a perfect love—"

"Stix." For so long, she'd desperately wanted him to talk. She still did. But it hurt.

He could see the hurt in her eyes, and his voice hushed. "There *was* no perfect love, Susan. That's what I'm trying to tell you. The emotions I felt for Kay were very sweet, very safe, very easy. Until I met you, I thought that was the best of what was possible. Until I met you, I defined the whole emotion of love on those parameters."

A log crashed in the fire. He never looked up. He tucked Susan more securely beneath him and held her. "If I'd loved her the right way, I would have gone after her. I never did because it wasn't that kind of love. What I felt was never worth the fight, the risk, the rejection. Nothing was worth being vulnerable for. Nothing was there to turn a man inside out and condense him into your basic caveman—possessive, protective, the-warrior-and-the-knight nonsense, shredding when I touch you, aching when I don't. Need, lust, laughter, loyalty, caring. *Love.* Like I feel for you."

Beneath him, he could feel her heart thumping like a drum. He smoothed a strand of hair from her cheek and shook his head at her expression. "You're looking scared, honey," he murmured softly. "You should be. Because it may have taken me a shamefully long time to figure out what love is, but I've got it down pat now. Believe me, Susan, there isn't a chance on this earth that I'll ever let you go."

Nine

——

When Susan first woke, it was very early. A pale, watery sun peered through the far dormer window. It took her a moment to recognize the slanted ceiling and massive mahogany four-poster of the loft.

The fire had died. The room was chilly, but she wasn't. Buried in a cuddle-warm nest of down comforters and goose-feather pillows, the only thing she lacked was Stix. He was gone.

Parts of her body still felt intimately tender from his lovemaking the night before. So did parts of her heart. A single night should not have the power to irrevocably change two people, but it had.

Karn's legacy had haunted her more than she knew. Even yesterday morning, she had been under the impression that she had ignorable physical needs, that she was a less-than-adequate sexual partner, that she was never likely to move a man to any heights, any depths.

Last night, Stix had shot those sure truths of hers straight to another galaxy. She curled into a ball, wanting to savor her secrets, her wonder; wishing there were a way to hold on to those moments. Honesty, though, intruded in the dim, silent room.

She had absolutely no regrets about having made love with him. Joy and love were swelling waves in her heart, but there was more to that ocean than moon-swept tides. Stix, too, had been affected by what had happened.

Last night had been like watching a man change in front of her eyes, climb out of his old emotional shell, grow, try, expand, open up. To her, Stix had always been a larger-than-life man. Now she knew him as an incomparably passionate lover and a vulnerable one.

He'd said he loved her.

She'd given him no response, and her silence now troubled her like an unpaid debt. They had both paid a heavy price in emotional interest for their ghosts. She knew Stix believed that those ghosts had been banished the night before. They had. But if last night had taught her anything at all, she had learned from the heart, from the soul, that she had a debt owing to Stix—and that the payment could not be postponed.

"What is this? You weren't planning on lazing around all morning, were you, Suze?"

She blinked at him, procrastinating honesty yet again. Standing in the arched doorway, he looked shamelessly bright-eyed and freshly showered. She had no idea he had a latent streak of cruelty until he crossed the room to the foot of the bed and deliberately, purposefully, started stealing the comforter.

"Hey! What time is it?"

"Seven."

When he tossed the comforter onto the floor, she clutched at the sheet. But his tug was stronger than her pull. "We haven't even had four hours' sleep!"

"I know. I have this horrible internal alarm clock that automatically rings at five. I'd planned on being slovenly and decadent and sleeping until six, but it just didn't go. Never mind that. You need to be up." Once he'd wrestled the sheet from her, she was stark bare. He could have looked repentant. He looked pleased. "It's cold up here," he observed.

Not when he looked at her. Not where he looked at her. "Come here, shorty." She used her best schoolmarm voice.

"Can't."

"Why not?"

"Because if I come over there you'll think I'm weak. You'll think I can't keep my hands off your body. You'll think I have no self-control, and that the look of your bare fanny moves me to blatant arousal. All of which is true, so I'm staying here until you have some clothes on. You can nap later, and I'll feed you later, but there's something you have to see."

"This had better be good," she said darkly, and swung her legs over the side of the bed. "Or I'm warning you—"

"Oh, good. A warning."

"This had better be good, or I'll trip you when you're least expecting it and tickle you senseless."

"Is that a promise or just cheap talk?"

He allotted her a fast five minutes to brush her teeth and throw on jeans, a shirt and a jacket. Then he ruthlessly pushed her out the back door. She shivered clear to her toes at that first blast of bright, frigid air, then totally forgot how sleepy, cold and hungry she was. For a short time, she even forgot all about debts of honesty.

Last night's rain had turned to ice, and the ice had created an irreplaceable and priceless fairyland. They walked his ravine, ultimately aiming for the lake.

High up, the glen was a blend of white pines and other conifers. Their branches were so heavily weighted with ice that the least touch of sunlight created prisms and rainbows. She couldn't turn without seeing a spectrum of emeralds, sapphires and rubies. Winter-hardy ferns hugged the forest floor, all coated with more crystal lace.

"See why I couldn't wait to wake you up?" Stix murmured.

"Yes." Both the illusion and reality had a terrible fragility, and perhaps adding to the specialness was knowing that the wonder of the fairy-tale world wouldn't last. The sun was out. The whole world was wet and dripping. In a matter of hours, his woods would just be woods again, not a lace-and-prism land for princesses.

Susan's earlier troubled mood returned to haunt her. She suddenly felt as fragile as the view. Nothing in nature was permanent. Even as nature created things of incomparable beauty, she set them up to change, not endure. Flowers wilted. Ice melted. And people who believed themselves indestructibly, powerfully, immutably in love found themselves mistaken.

Stix took her hand, leading her down the steep incline to the lake. "There's bluebonnets and hummingbirds in summer, and the fish cuddle in this cove, just begging for someone to toss in a line."

Ice crunched beneath her boots as they left the dark magic woods for the sunlit shoreline. She thought she knew the lake. Some said Coeur d'Alene was the most beautiful lake in the Northwest. She'd seen the sailing races on it one summer and she'd seen massive timber logs being transported on it in the fall, but she'd never seen the Coeur as she saw it now.

Stix's cove was like a place out of time. No one had developed the land here. No sounds intruded into the stillness. No buildings, no roads or boats or chimneys interrupted the landscape. Jutting slopes of land fingered to the shore, making it uniquely a mountain lake with a feel of sprawling wildness and privacy. The water foamed at the rocky shore's edge, clear and clean, an icy blue.

"You like it, Suze?" Stix perched on a waist-high smooth boulder.

"More than 'like.' Did you swim here as a kid?" She took the flatter stone next to him and swung up her legs so the frothy little waves couldn't catch her.

"Sometimes, when I was in a masochistic mood. The water will freeze your toes off on the hottest day."

"You spent summers here, though?"

"Most of them. Hiking the ravine edge, building tree houses. Raised a family of raccoons and was bitten by an opossum once. The result was thirteen shots direct in the belly for the threat of rabies, which my dad said would teach me a lesson. It didn't. I still picked up any live thing that would let me. When I was nine and ten, it took me all summer to build cages, which were a total waste. I never held on to a wild thing for long—it wouldn't have been right—I just wanted to catch them and make friends and let them go again." He hesitated. "You getting hungry?"

"No," she said impatiently. She was starved, but Stix was talking. She hungered to hear him talk far more than she'd ever needed food. "What about after you got a little older?"

He shrugged. "I worked for my dad. Got good with an ax, a chain saw, chains, forklifts, earth movers. Drove a semi for him for a couple of summers." He grinned lazily. "You load up a semitrailer with a few tons of logs and head up and down a few steep mountain roads and I'll show you what some real fear is."

"Scary stuff?"

"I can remember one time my brakes burned out halfway down a three-mile fifteen-percent mountain grade. I'd never touched the gas and my speedometer was gaining sixty; I had forty tons of momentum behind me and there weren't any side rails between me and a thousand-foot drop."

"I don't know what you did, but I'll tell you what I would have done."

"What?"

"Wet my pants," she said wryly. He chuckled, and then so did she. But again she thought of the kind of father who would demand his son face danger. And she thought of a man—*her* man—who never paraded his courage. He simply had it.

Stix lurched up from his rock and leaned over her. He pulled her gloved hands around his neck and homed in for a kiss. The crisp air had put a cherry on her nose and her eyes were bright in the sunlight. They'd been bright all morning. Too bright.

She willingly lifted to her feet—actually to tiptoe—and her lips were pliant and supple and yielding under his, but that worried him, too. Susan was not by nature a pliant lamb, and the Lord knew she was never quiet. Talking wasn't the same thing as *talking*.

Her only response to his declaration the night before had occurred in passion, and she'd made love with him that third time as if he were the last life raft in the Pacific. Desperation and fierceness had flavored her kisses. A blind searching had flavored her touch. She'd slept clinging, holding tightly, as if she were positive he'd disappear in the night.

He wasn't going to disappear, but he didn't know how to bridge that determined, showy smile of hers. He told her he was making her breakfast.

"Oh, no, you're not," she said severely. "I admit I've gone out of my way to appear klutzy in a kitchen. You're intimidating, shorty, because you're so good in one. But that's half the point. You're *always* stuck cooking breakfast at the restaurant. This time you relax."

When her pancakes burned, she served him cereal with milk. "It's your stove," she insisted. "There's something wrong with that burner. It's too hot."

"There's nothing wrong with the burner. It's your attitude," he teased her. "Poor baby, you grew up on women's lib. You just can't get rid of the idea that cooking's a demeaning and tiresome drudgery. Didn't you know you could have fun in a kitchen?"

She got the picture when he sang in an operatic baritone while washing the dishes, also when he descended on her with soapy, dripping hands for a kiss. Not a regular kiss but one of those kinds that wouldn't wait.

She scolded him. "You've become insatiable. Tyrannical, dictatorial, bossy, domineering, greedy—"

"If you don't get your hands out of my front pockets, lady, you're going to directly discover what I've become, but in the meantime..." He nibbled on her left ear long enough to make her squirm. She squirmed, but she didn't move, and her fingers continued to tease inside his pockets. Occasionally Susan completely forgot that she was a stable, serious, responsible anthropology professor. She even forgot to look so desperately worried, and he wasn't about to remind her. He continued the assault on her earlobe.

"We have choices ahead of us. We can go share a shower and a nap—and heaven knows, we didn't get much sleep last night. Or we can head into town and go wander around Tubbs Hill and Fort Sherman and the park and—I don't believe I'm saying this—the shopping district."

"I have a better choice." She suddenly pulled away from him, but no farther than arm's length.

"So do I."

"Not *that*. I swear you have a vampire streak, except that you don't wait for nightfall." She smiled up at him, but her eyes were serious and she carefully chose her words. "I understood what you said about your father, the reasons you haven't spent time here, Stix. But don't you think your point's long been made? This place is too special to be deserted for so long."

"Maybe." He added, "Maybe that's even partly why I wanted you to see it. But yesterday you weren't calling it too 'special.' In fact, I didn't think you liked it at all."

"Because I thought it was haunted by bad memories for you."

He shook his head. "Bad and good memories are stored in the mind, Suze."

"You can store good memories in a place with a little effort."

"What did you have in mind?"

Four hours later, he was sorry he'd asked. Susan had in mind cleaning cupboards, rearranging furniture, moving out the bar, moving in an old chest she found in the garage, and above all and everything, making all the stuffed animal heads disappear.

"This nesting instinct related to the genetic flaw you have for shopping?" he asked patiently.

"Where's a ladder? That caretaker of yours hasn't dusted a ceiling in years. Look at that cobweb! Stix, head for the trestle table in the dining ell. If you take out a few of those leaves, two people could see each other from opposite ends without binoculars." She looked at him—her filthy hands on filthy, blue-jeaned hips—blew a strand of hair from her forehead and crowed, "This place is so beautiful! You're going to love it when we're finished."

He didn't have to love the place. He loved her, and waves of the emotion kept engulfing him, like when he saw Susan pass by him with a bucket of soapy water; and when she climbed down from the ladder yelling because a live spider had dropped into her hair; and when he found her in the kitchen, the entire upper part of her body stuck in a bottom cupboard, with her fanny wagging enticingly in his direction.

To Susan, what made a home was cleanliness, the sweep of possessions that had private value, and the stamps of color and mood that made up a personal feeling of belonging.

He saw home as Susan.

On his way out the back door with the massive bear head from the bathroom, he said, "You're sure you want this gone? What if our children want to brush their teeth looking at the bear?"

She let it by.

When they sat on the counter between toolboxes and debris, eating sandwiches at the speed of light and gulping ice-cold cider, he said, "I figured you've set this whole thing up as a premarriage test, right? You don't care that I love you a skyful, Suze. What really turns you on is a man who has the muscle to lift a wall—obediently."

She leapt on that word "obediently," but let the reference to marriage fly on by.

She found a leaky fixture in the upstairs bathroom sink. While he was flat on his back under the drainpipe elbow, she handed him wrenches with the precision of the nurse portion of a surgeon's team. In fact, she gave him so much help that it took him twice the time. He said, "The black and white's a little stark in here. What color do you want to do it over, Suze?"

She muttered, "What do you have all these wrenches for if you only need one?" and let it slide.

Susan let a lot by, until dinner was over and the sun had set and a fresh fire blazed in the living-room hearth. The living room looked different by then.

She'd thrown open draperies to let in light, and warmth had naturally appeared once the rifle cabinet and trophies were gone. The furniture was no longer stacked against walls but clustered around the hearth, because Stix loved a fire. He also didn't need coffee tables cluttering up space for his knees. The walls still needed something—not paintings, but something with texture and fabric to bring warmth to the stone. But those choices would come. For now, she'd simply wanted to give Stix a place that belonged to him, a room he could be comfortable and easy and happy in.

It was all she could give him.

Except for humor. "Quit groaning, shorty. I'm not killing you."

"I thought when you offered a back rub you were going to *soothe* the muscles, not beat them."

"You should be happy I take my back rubs seriously."

"I was, until I realized who taught you the fine art of massage, Suze: Attila the Hun."

She would have smiled any other time. Stix played enough basketball and racquetball to be in terrific physical condition, but a long day of carrying and lifting had stressed unfamiliar muscles. She knew he was sore and that he was sore because of her. So she had every intention of taking care of him.

More than he knew. Her eyes softened as she worked and kneaded the kinks in his back. She'd banished all the dead critters except for the big white polar-bear rug he was lying on. She knew Stix believed she had a feminine, irrational aversion to those trophies, and she'd let him keep thinking that. The truth was that she'd wanted them gone for his sake, so the room could have no unconscious associations with his father's values and his own harsh childhood memories. But the polar bear was different; they'd made it different last night.

His skin, a smooth, supple bronze, contrasted with the coarse white fur of the rug. He was still wet-haired from a recent shower, and a towel was loosely hooked around his waist as he lay on his stomach. With every stroke, she memorized the look of him, the feel of him—her love of him.

Her head was just as damp from her own shower, but she'd thrown on one of his T-shirts. The fabric flopped at her thighs and hung to her elbows, unnoticed, just as she ignored the smothering creep of exhaustion. Sleep would never happen, she knew—not until she did what had to be done.

All day she'd heard him sneak in the little teasing comments about marriage and children. All day, *I'll never let you go* had lingered in her mind. And all day, she'd come closer and closer to tears.

She couldn't remember the last time she'd cried, and she had no intention of letting Stix see that happen now. She applied more oil to her hands and rubbed harder. "If anybody ever takes you for a spy, shorty, tell them not to waste any fancy tortures on you. Give you a back rub and you'll tell anybody anything they want to know."

"Do not," he murmured, "make insulting slurs on my honor when I'm comatose."

"When we go home tomorrow, it has to be like it was." She'd hoped to slip that into the conversation easily, but it didn't work. As if he'd been waiting for the sound of a rifle cock, every muscle in his body tensed. "We're good friends, Stix," she said softly. "Being lovers one time doesn't change that."

"You're wrong. Being lovers has changed everything. And you know it, Susan." He twisted around and coiled to a sitting position. One look, and she knew he wasn't going to listen, and that she wasn't going to be able to handle this well. Again, she had the sensation that he'd been waiting for this. His shoulders, still glistening with oil, were rigid; his jaw set and his gaze as deep as love, as raw as anger. "In thirty seconds flat I can show you that 'good friends' is not what you feel for me. Nor is it remotely what I feel for you."

She fought for calm. "You're talking about sex—"

"You bet I am. Along with watching you grow big as a boat with each of our kids. And buying a matched set of canes when we're old enough to have arthritis." He searched her face. "I told you about Kay. You can't still believe—"

"No. I believe what you said. You're over her. I even believe you feel love for me." She took a huge breath, to still her fingers from trembling, to force a common-sense resonance into her tone. "What I don't believe is that your feelings will last." She tried a smile. "Come on, shorty, when you come out of a dark cave after a long time, any light feels good. That's all that's happening. When you haven't played with love in a long time, nature jumps in there with a giant dose of phenylethylamine. You heard me give a lecture on that chemical, once. It's real. It's real and it's powerful and it's wonderful, but it wears off. It *always* wears off."

"Susan, I don't give a hoot about your nine-syllable chemical and we're not talking about anything that's going to wear off." But he lowered his voice, looking at her. Her hair was drying in feathery wisps around her cheeks. She was swallowing, hard. By firelight her eyes were golden brown with a glisten, and so damn hopeless. "I *love* you," he said fiercely. "And you're not going to tell me that you don't love me, because I know better. I made love with you last night. I know the way you look at me, the way you are with me."

"No." Control was suddenly hanging by a thread from a cliff edge, a parachute with a stuck ripcord. She couldn't think when he looked at her that way, and the words suddenly tumbled out, blind, desperate. "I think something died in me a long time ago. Trust? Vulnerability? All I know is that I've lost my ability to believe in tomorrows, and that I'm not going to risk failing you. If we can't go back to 'friends,' Stix, we can't go on at all."

When she tried to rise, his big hands clamped on her wrists. Through a web of tears, all she could see were his bottomless dark eyes. His voice was low, urgent. "You think I didn't know this was coming? But not like this, Susan, not all mixed up with biology and failures and trust and tomorrows, as if that's all supposed to make sense. It doesn't. You're going to have to tell me what you're afraid of."

"I'm not afraid. This has nothing to do with fear—"

"To hell it doesn't. Now talk to me."

"I *am* talking to you. I'm trying to tell you that I'm getting out of your life—"

"Talk to me!"

She shook when he raised his voice. She should have known that it was all thunder and no storm, but at that moment, he didn't care what she thought, as long as she reacted. And that she did. Her face turned white and suddenly there was a torrential flood of words, stories, emotions, pain. She talked so low and fast that he could barely hear, and she didn't begin to wear down until she'd spilled out one last crazy story. It was something about being sent to a foster-parent couple when she was five, about her desperately trying to be good, about their sending her back. They'd wanted a dark-haired child because they were dark-haired. "I had the wrong hair color! Now do you understand?"

He didn't understand a damn thing except that Susan had dammed up about five thousand memories for far too long, that she had a nasty habit of blaming herself for the wrong things, that hurt was exploding from her—and that to her, it all added up to a reason for leaving him.

Nothing really added up at all, but convincing her of that was out of the question. She was being brick-wall stubborn and she was crying. So he did the only thing he knew how to do: hold her. He gathered her up, tightly and closely, and when she gradually gained an ounce of emotional control, he crushed her mouth under his. Softly. Fiercely. With anger and frustration and tenderness and love. With everything he had.

Expecting resistance, he found none. Expecting to force her into believing in what they had, he found no need for force. Her mouth yielded under his—warm, pliant, mobile. She arched her throat so he could take anything he wanted. She cushioned his frustration with a woman's weapons: fragrance, warmth, giving, passion.

But when he lifted his head, his eyes dazed and confused, her voice was finally steady again—too steady, too strong. "That's why. That's why I'm not going to risk hurting you more than I already have. You're finally over a relationship that tore you up for years. The last thing you need is to get involved in another one that has no chance of working out."

He could have argued that nonsense, and started to when she threw him a bullet that penetrated low and hard. She delivered it with a lioness's fierce tenderness for her mate. But his old nemesis was rejection. It hit him exactly where it hurt, and stopped him cold.

She said softly, "Stix, I just don't love you. There's nothing more to say."

A bell tinkled when he opened the florist's door. Brushing flakes of snow from his hair, Stix strode for the counter and reached for the checkbook in his back pocket. Mrs. McCarthy peered out from the back room and immediately hustled toward him. This week her hair was blue. Last week she'd had a pink rinse. "Afternoon, Stix! Come in to pay your account?"

"Yes."

She always wet her pencil with her tongue before writing out the receipt and smiled at him with an honorary grandmother's possessiveness. "Same order for next week?"

"Yes."

"Red roses are a better bargain than peach—"

"I just want the peach."

"And that's fine." She took his check and waived his offer to produce ID. "Forecast for more snow. I suppose we have to expect that in late January. Everyone who comes in is crabby. I declare we're all tired of the gray days." She smiled at him, and just as if she were still discussing the weather, continued, "She'll come around, Stix. Don't you worry. A woman always comes around for roses."

He had a bill to pay at the baker for a standing weekly order of Sin Cake. Joe told him, "She's a good girl. Too many girls are easy these days. You wouldn't want that, would you? Next week we could try napoleons."

The bookstore—Book People—had his seven ordered volumes of poetry waiting for him. The owner, thankfully, didn't say a word about Susan, although the salesclerk—unasked—had wrapped the bundle in peach paper with a bow. Several times in the past month, Stix had considered moving to New York, Tokyo, London. Any place big. Any place where people didn't know him.

Now, though, with his business done on Main Street, he climbed into his car and drove the slushy streets toward the mall. Within fifteen minutes he was under cover, warm, dry, and appallingly nervous. His hands were wet, his throat dry. He could not believe how many women's stores there were, and he had no idea what he was doing.

That last feeling was familiar. He hadn't known what he was doing for weeks. All his life, he'd had a holy terror of rejection. Susan had clearly rejected him. How do you get any clearer than *I just don't love you*? And when a woman didn't love a man, he was supposed to back off.

He not only hadn't backed off; he'd the same as invited the whole town to witness his humiliation. The roses hadn't moved her, neither had the baker's best temptations, the poetry, the hand-varnished toboggan with the silver bow. If none of that had touched her, it was a cinch she wasn't going to be moved by *this*.

"Never thought I'd see you in here, Stix. Could I help you with something?"

He'd counted on—prayed for—a little anonymity at the mall, but the buxom woman with the spit bangs and wholesome smile was unquestionably Harvey's wife. Her husband was a regular at the restaurant every morning. "I'm just looking," he said sternly.

"You're sure you don't need a little help?"

"Positive."

But he did. He had no idea the lingerie section would be so complicated. He knew he wanted something slinky and soft and sexy, but there were whole tables of slinky, soft, sexy stuff. It all looked alike. He couldn't move without running into mannequin breasts. And there were other shoppers—women who looked at him. He had nowhere to hide.

"Stix." Harvey's wife was suddenly back at his side, her smile so patient that he was thoroughly annoyed.

"Sweetheart, you see that teddy you have in your hands?"

It wasn't in his hands anymore. He'd dropped it.

"It's very nice, Stix, very pretty," she said soothingly, "but it would fit me. If you'll take a very quick peek just below my neck, I think you can figure out awfully fast that it doesn't have a horse's hair chance of fitting Susan. Could you try and trust me? I've talked more men through this than you can believe. Let's start out with color...."

She waited expectantly. He murmured, really low, "Red."

"Red? You're sure you wouldn't prefer one of the softer pastels? Or basic black?"

The darn woman had a helluva voice on her. His stayed even with a whisper. "It has to be red."

"Well, that'll make it a little tougher, but we'll manage. Now, are we talking camisoles? Teddies? Nightgowns? Bra-and-pantie sets?"

He wondered fleetingly if there was a fire escape. More than that, he wished for a fire. Quickly.

The shopping wasn't so tough. It was watching himself suffer through it for absolutely nothing. He'd known before he started the gift campaign that it wasn't going to do any good. Presents were never likely to work with Suze. They were just his way of letting her know he was still around—and intended to stay around until he figured out what *would* work.

That was tricky. Some might even call it impossible. Once he'd put together all the puzzle pieces, all the scraps and hints and secrets she'd ever thrown at him, he had the nature of the beast that haunted her.

Susan had an awfully hard time believing in Susan. Everyone she'd ever loved had walked away from her, turned their backs, chosen or wanted someone else when it came down to the crunch. She thought that was going to happen again. She was waiting for it to happen again.

Stix had figured out that much. Just not what to do about it. How did you make a woman believe in herself, in reaching out for what she felt, what she wanted? How did you make her believe that no one was walking out on her this time? How could you make a woman believe in the future when she was too damned scared to try?

And there was always the possibility that she'd meant what she said. He woke up daily with the choice of believing that. Or the choice of continuing to act like a lovesick fool with no pride or sense, flying blind, wasting energy. A year ago he'd had some sanity and a lot of sensitivity about rejection.

A year ago he hadn't met Susan, and when it came down to it, it was her fault he was in this mess. She was the one who'd changed his view of himself as a man—the man he was, the man he wanted to be, the man he was capable of becoming.

With her.

It had to be with her. Because not a damn thing made sense without her.

He had to do better than red satin camisoles. And he intended to—the very instant he figured out how to make her believe in tomorrow, and in him, and most of all: in Susan.

Ten

Susan stepped off the scales, ten pounds lighter than she had been a month and a half before. For five years she'd been trying to get those pounds off her thighs. Snap her fingers, lose Stix, and without any effort she was model svelte and slim.

She pushed the towel around the steam-smudged bathroom mirror and caught a glimpse of herself. *You also have a face the color of a corpse, Markham. Maybe you'd better start eating again. And sleeping. The circles under your eyes are bigger than boats.*

She turned away and pulled on a robe. The agenda for the evening was preparing essay questions for midterms. Barefoot, she prowled the house for the textbooks she wanted, all the while trying to prop up her mood with the counting-blessings maxim. She was holding down a job. She had good and caring friends. She'd just earned a raise and had a roof over her head.

Good God, people were starving in Africa. She had everything.

Except Stix.

The loss was her own doing—something that she never forgot and never forgave. Some nights, the bite of honesty soothed her sense of grieving. He'd needed someone to help him over Kay. She had, but she also knew that what Stix had felt for her had been the first taste of emotion after a long drought. You can't hold a thirsty man just because you're the first woman to offer him water.

Other nights, she was not prepared to be so rational. Those nights she lay awake and alone, aching with the thought that she'd thrown away the only man she'd ever really loved, the only man who'd seemed to love her. It was always the word *seemed* that stopped her from calling him. She'd trusted that illusion before—and lost every time. When she'd trusted her emotions before, she'd been wrong. Every time.

She'd glued back all the broken pieces before, but it wasn't the same with Stix. He was more. He meant more. And she'd come far too close to something she knew was inexorably linked to her own emotional survival.

It should have been better after last week. He'd stopped sending the roses. He'd stopped sending the poetry and the bakery's confections. He'd stopped sending everything. She'd known that would happen. She'd been waiting for it. He'd given up. Which was exactly what she'd asked for, exactly what she wanted.

So pull yourself out of the pit, Markham. You're as much fun to live with as a ghost.

She was trying. She particularly spent the next minutes trying. The phone jangled just as she was piling a legal pad and textbook on the desk. She tucked the receiver between her ear and shoulder as she continued to rearrange the night's work. "Hello?" Her tone was distracted. She couldn't find a pencil. Six red pens, but no pencil. Yesterday she would have stood on her head for a red pen.

"It's Stix, Susan."

A rush of heat flushed through her body at the sound of his voice. Yearning, like the bleat of a lost shepherd's lamb on a hillside, filled up her throat.

"You there?"

She cleared her throat. "Yes." *Markham, you have to do better than that. Much better.* "How have you been?"

"Fine. I just called to ask you something."

His tone was as mellow as a spring wind, casual, easy. It hurt. It almost hurt so much that she missed what he was asking, and then his request was so unexpected and prosaic that she felt loss all over again.

He was only calling about some cave. They'd talked about their mutual hobby before, but never shared a spelunking experience. Long before they'd met each other, both had gone in their own directions to find fellow cavers, as there were so few around Moscow. What he wanted was for her to spend a few hours Saturday exploring a particular cave north of the Palouse country.

"The thing is that the property's about to be sold, so the chance to explore it is now or never," he told her. "I have two men I usually go with, but neither of them could work out for Saturday. You don't go caving alone, particularly in unfamiliar territory—"

"No, no, of course not." Even a careless spelunker never broke that cardinal rule.

There was a long pause at the other end of the line. "Susan, I didn't call to put you on the spot. I've accepted how you feel. In fact, that's partly why I called. Moscow's too small; I don't want you to feel you have to avoid running into me. And I thought an outing like this might make that easier. I know you like spelunking—there was no way I could go without a spotter—and caving's just...caving."

She knew. There was nothing romantic about miner's helmets and rappelling hooks and bats, and she couldn't keep clutching up every time she caught sight of him on Main Street. A chance to see him and act normally was the chance to get her life under control again.

There was no reason not to accept. His whole invitation was laid out in the most casual manner. It was just an offer. Nothing more. He was over her. Well over her. He wasn't even calling her Suze anymore.

She was glad. If he'd called her Suze, she would probably have done something totally idiotic, like burst into tears.

"So, what do you think? Is your schedule real busy on Saturday?"

Her schedule was packed, because she'd worked very hard to pack it. Saturday's list included a lunch date with a fellow professor, a haircut scheduled for three in the afternoon, and a few students who had asked to come over for the evening. "This Saturday?"

"This Saturday," he repeated. "Say, around eight. We'll need an early start. It's quite a drive."

"Quite a drive" turned into almost three hours, although Susan couldn't have said where, when, or how they'd finally arrived in this backwoods mountain country. Stix hadn't been tense but she had been. He'd done all the talking and she'd done all the looking. His denim jacket and jeans fit his body like old friends. His face had healthy color and his eyes were brown, alert and alive. He surely didn't look like a man who'd been pining.

"We'd better repack our gear before we go in. From what I've heard, the cave is a real labyrinth of passages."

"Fine." She felt a little easier, once they were out of the car and moving. The sky, ground and trees were all a late-winter dull gray. The wind was bitter and the air damp. Just beyond where Stix had dropped all the gear to reorganize, she could see the narrow cave-opening, cloaked in brush. "You said you hadn't been here before?"

"Never," Stix lied. "But people have been telling me about it for years. She's supposed to be tricky—some tight squeezes and several long drops. There's supposed to be a vein of silver in one cavern. And an underground river."

She had to smile. "Sounds like a fisherman's story to me. Most caves don't get that fancy in this part of the world. We're hardly in Kentucky-Tennessee cave country here."

"That's where you apprenticed?"

"Yes. It wasn't that far a drive from Indianapolis."

"I started spelunking in Utah, then a little in southern Idaho. Regardless, probably what I heard about this cave was greatly exaggerated. But it sure pricked my interest."

"Mine, too." Susan bent down to clamp the knee-pads over her jeans.

"Hey, you've got that seat harness all tangled." He ambled behind her, where she was trying to adjust the canvas straps that fit over her jacket like suspenders. She felt his hands skim her shoulders as he straightened the tangled harness. Every nerve ending instantly become electric, aware. She could smell his skin, his clean hair. She could taste her wanting for him.

And she could feel exactly how casual and impersonal his touch was.

"It's starting to snow. Let's finish the rest of this under cover. There's too much we don't want to get wet."

She nodded, and ducked through the brush into the narrow cave-opening. Inside it was dark—but a long way from the pitch black of true underground—and immediately warmer. She dropped her loose pack and supplies and turned on the battery lantern so Stix could see to finish sorting through their gear. Pulling on her helmet, she glanced around the cave's first chamber. There wasn't much to see, until she looked up about ten feet and noticed the covey of bats hanging upside down, ten feet up. "I used to be terrified of bats, until I realized how many unfair stereotypes we have of them," she admitted.

"Like what?" He noticed where she was looking, and then concentrated on attaching his nylon safety line to her belt, which was the best excuse he had to keep his hands on her.

"You know. Like the old stereotype about bats carrying rabies.... That was never true. Very few contract rabies, and they're almost never aggressive."

"I've heard that." His hand barely brushed hers. He noticed her cheeks took on fevered color, but he'd run out of excuses to fuss with the safety line.

"And there's the other silly myth about how bats fly for a woman's hair. It's pretty obvious if a bat can pluck up a tiny mosquito in midair, it can sure as heck make out anything as big as a woman's head." She glanced at him. "They avoid people like the plague. They don't bother anyone."

"Didn't realize." He moved from his caver's pack to hers and redistributed supplies for weight. She could carry both superinsulating survival blankets because they were light, while he stuffed his pack with the heavier items, such as the canteens and spare batteries and minor repair tools for their carbide lights.

"Bats are clean. And they're gentle animals. And although some species are hopeless philanderers, there are lots of bats who make devoted lovers. They can't tolerate the least separation. They're really very sweet."

"Susan?" Stix murmured.

"What?"

"I don't know why you don't just admit they scare the wits out of you."

She looked startled and then chuckled, the first honest chuckle he'd heard from her so far today. "Darn it, I've *tried* to like them," she said wryly.

"You don't have to try too hard. They're hibernating to beat the band. Now, you can do the honors leading, but let's take some extra precautions against getting lost." Making sure Susan noticed, he attached a spool of nylon string to his belt, then anchored the loose end to a rock at the cave opening. The string would unravel, making a Hansel-and-Gretel-like trail back home. "You brought chalk?"

"Lots, in my pocket."

"So you mark where we go. And Susan? You get tired, we stop. You get in trouble, you don't fuss around. You say so early. And you use the safety line for every descent."

Caution and cooperation were the unwritten laws of caving. By stating the rules, though, Stix had automatically established himself as chief honcho, and that was another unwritten caving law. Two votes of fifty-fifty were ineffective in a crisis, so one spelunker was always voted leader. Usually it was the one implicitly trusted by the others, the one whose experience and judgment were the most valued.

In every group Susan had been involved in underground, she had been the leader. That she automatically allowed Stix that right and power over her told her something, though it was nothing she didn't already know: she trusted him, she valued him. Dammit, she loved him.... But she immediately forced her mind back to the task at hand.

Twenty yards in, the temperature warmed and the first cavern squeezed to a narrow crawl space. Midpassage she marked the spot with chalk, scuttled through another several feet on hands and knees, then tested a drop-off for depth. They both chimneyed down the short ten feet, and below, her helmet light illuminated a choice of three tunneling passages.

If she could have kept her thoughts off the man just behind her, she would automatically have been feeling the catch of intrigue. A good cave, a deep cave, was loaded with life, and what had first drawn her to spelunking were the mysterious creatures that survived in a cave. Nothing should have been able to live without light, and without a visible food source. Yet the cave creatures did, coming as close to a self-contained survival system as existed in nature. That principle appealed to the biological anthropologist—and to the woman—in Susan. With enough will and determination, one could survive on almost nothing.

Until she'd pushed Stix out of her life six weeks ago, she'd believed that undeniable, irrefutable biological truth without a single doubt. At the moment, she'd happily sacrifice will, determination and her entire character for a chance to hold him. But again, she forced emotion away and demanded concentration of herself.

She took the right fork, marking it with chalk, and edged her way along a narrow wall for several yards. They were in true darkness now. The wall turned into a narrow ledge and her headlight illuminated an unpleasant, sharp drop. Water dribbled from places in the wall. The ledge was slick. "I may be leading us toward a dead end," she called back to Stix.

"Could be. If that happens, we'll try one of the other passages."

"There's fresh air, are you noticing? But I can't locate the source. There's no hint of light. I'll be darned. Here's another fork!"

"The left one looks kind of interesting."

"Okay, left it is." She marked it.

Stix erased her chalk mark, just as he'd erased all the others, and followed after her—an ascending left turn, a descending right, and then he carefully coaxed her right again.

"I had no idea there were caves this big in the area! *Stix!* Look at this!"

He duly admired the trickling stream she'd come across. Crouched on the stone shore, she shone the flashlight on the tiny, almost-transparent fish schooling in the stream. He thought she'd like them, but almost immediately she was on her feet again. He talked

her into a lunch break—just sandwiches and coffee
from a thermos, eaten standing up—but Susan definitely didn't want to linger. Not where he was close
enough to really look at her. Not where he was close
enough to touch.

She beamed her flashlight in a full circle. "I can't
believe we have another choice of two passages. What
a maze this place is turning into! The left passage an-
gling up looks the most interesting, although I'd better
make larger chalk marks if we're going any farther."

"Good idea," Stix agreed, and the moment she
moved ahead, snipped off the spool of nylon string behind them. Guiding her was tricky. Susan *did* have a
mind of her own, and he had to watch which direction
she took as well as maintain enough distance to unob-
trusively erase her chalk marks.

She also moved very hard and very fast. He understood why. Safety in a cave took intense concentration.
The harder and more physical the exercise, the more the
mind emptied of distractions, emotions. He knew what
she was doing. He just hoped that he knew what *he* was
doing.

One crawl space took them forever to travel; all their
gear had to be pushed ahead of them. Then they
climbed a winding, sharp-edged tunnel. She almost
took a wrong turn, but he coaxed her left. When she
first missed the bright gleam on the walls, he vaguely
aimed his flashlight so she'd notice.

"Stix! I don't believe this!"

"What?"

She plucked off her gloves with excitement. The cave
walls were of rough, gritty stone, except for a thin,
narrow streak of silver. Real silver. Soft, moldable,
preciously bright silver. "It's *real*, isn't it?"

"Looks it."

"But we're not north enough to be near Idaho's real silver country, are we?"

He shrugged, innocent as a three-year-old caught with his hand in a cookie jar. "You want to follow the vein?"

Wild horses couldn't have stopped her from following the vein. Stix could have told her that sooner or later, if you dug into a mountain in Idaho, you'd find silver. The trick wasn't finding the metal, but discovering a lode that was commercially viable and safe to mine. Right now, he knew Suze didn't want to hear about commercial viability. The gleam, the beauty and the softness of the silver drew her, and she looked fiercely disappointed when "her" vein petered out in a dead-end wall.

"But maybe we'll pick it up again if we can find a way around the other side," he suggested.

"Assuming there is another side to that wall." She sighed. "Maybe we'd better get realistic here. This is the most special cave I've found in years! But Stix, we've already been going for hours. I have no idea what time it is—"

"Early yet," he said quickly.

"You think we still have time—?"

"Sure."

They chimneyed down a short decline, squinched through a backbender of a narrow tunnel, and then he had her, in the cavern he called The Silver Room.

He'd been spelunking for years and never found a chamber like it. The space was roughly twelve by fourteen, and the walls peaked to a pyramid shape. Fresh air drafted in from the point, but the appeal of the cavern room was its silver—not skinny veins, but whole ledges of it. The barest headlight picked up the glow and sheen of the metal, spanning the width and entire breadth of the chamber. Susan was entranced. He'd hoped she would be.

And in due time, she was terrified.

He'd hoped she would be.

"I didn't realize there were three tunnels leading into here when we crawled through—and I'll be darned if they don't look completely identical." Her voice was still light, still calm, even when she gave up burrowing a few feet into the varying tunnels and looked at him. "Stix, I can't find my chalk mark."

"It's there. I saw you make it. We'll both look."

They both looked. There were, miraculously, no chalk marks. "It's not like there's a problem," she said cheerfully. "All we have to do is follow your nylon thread—"

"Damn!"

"Damn," she echoed faintly.

He shook his head. "One of those last down-scale passages had some rough sides. I heard the thread scraping but never realized she was wearing through."

Her fingertips turned to ice. Stix might be the unspoken boss and he'd had the thread, but she'd never trusted spooled thread as a direction finder. No matter how strong it was, thread broke easily. She'd taken the lead. She'd had the chalk. She was the one responsible for knowing where they were going, but memories of a dozen twists and turns confused in her mind. And she knew why.

Her mind had been on the man, not the cave. That was an unforgivable break of the rules. A caver was supposed to keep her mind on the cave even if she broke all four limbs. She knew that. She also knew that it was a huge, big black cave to be lost in. No one would ever hear them if they yelled. No one even knew they were here.

She wound her arms around her chest. "When we first came in here, what did you see? Was that jutting ledge on the right or the left?"

"I think it was on the right."

"I think it was on the left." Fear, invidious as a poison, seeped into her tone. "There is absolutely nothing to panic about. All we have to do is try all three tunnels and keep going until we find something familiar." She just couldn't stop thinking that she'd already checked several feet into all three. Triplets should look so much alike, and certain caves were monsters of look-alike passages. "It probably won't take long at all. It's just... We've already been on the go for hours. You have to be tired; I know I am. And exhaustion magnifies in a cave. You start making mistakes."

"So we take a rest and think this through." Gently he unhooked her caver's pack, then his, then started detaching all the lines and harnesses and extra gear. She moved as quickly as he did. He unfolded one of the survival blankets to give them a place to sit. She foraged for candles, lit one, and then switched off their carbide headlights because that source of illumination was too valuable to waste.

"I was always taught that the best way out of a crisis situation is to prepare for the worst," Stix said.

"Yes, I'm already going through the light sources. We have the carbides—" she pushed off her jacket "—three candles each, six books of matches. You have the lantern; we both have flashlights."

"So we're fine that way for a while. How about food?" He watched her rummage through their packs.

"If you're fond of raisins and snack packs and chocolate, we're not going to starve for a day. The thermos
is still half filled with coffee; we both have a canteen of
water." Everything she found was extremely reassur-
ing. She couldn't imagine why the thread of panic kept
creeping into her tone. It had nothing to do with food
or water. She said suddenly, fiercely, "Stix, nothing's
going to happen to you. Nothing."

He saw the look in her eyes. "Come here, Susan."

"Do you want coffee?"

"I want you to come here."

He'd already dropped to the blanket, stretched out
his legs, half unzipped his jacket. She knelt next to him,
and the blanket was so narrow that she was suddenly as
close as a heartbeat. She could see the smudge of dirt on
his cheek, where his hair had matted down under the
miner's hat.

She'd carefully avoided being this close to him this
far. She'd carefully avoided letting her thoughts drift to
thinking what a fine, beautiful man he was. She'd
carefully avoided the tendrils of need sneaking through
her veins. She'd carefully avoided looking at his mouth,
his eyes.

"You're afraid," he said gently. "And the only way
I know to work with fear is to think through the worst
things that could happen. And then deal with them. In
the worst possible scenario, we would have no air, no
water, no food. But we have those."

"Yes."

"There could be a cave-in."

"Yes."

"One of us could be hurt or injured."

"Yes."

"Or in another 'worst possible scenario,' we could be lost here forever. Never find our way out."

Her "Yes" that time never got said. Her ears took in his words, but her heart was listening to something else. Like a lonely coyote's bay for the moon, she suddenly heard the silent howl of unbearable loneliness and yearning.

He wanted her to think about worst scenarios and survival. She was. The worst scenario she could think of was a world without Stix. And true survival, she was terribly afraid, had nothing to do with cave-ins or food supplies. It had to do with him.

Nothing had been right since she'd left him. She loved him more than life, and the Lord knew she had the terrible habit of losing everything that had ever mattered to her. She thought she'd faced up to those losses. She just couldn't seem to face up to this one. There simply was no survival without him—not any kind of survival that mattered.

"Suze?" She hadn't heard that nickname in a very long time. The way he said it made her toes curl, and it made her think of rhythm and blues. She loved rhythm and blues. "Honey, there is absolutely nothing to be afraid of. But I think you're already starting to figure that out, aren't you?"

He picked up one of her limp arms and hooked it around his neck. "In the absolutely worst scenario you could possibly think of, you'd be alone and lost," he said softly. "But you have to believe me, love. I'd find you. Every time."

Lazy, like a man who had nothing better to do, he dropped his mouth on hers. The kiss was as soft as the brush of a butterfly's wing, as irrevocable as promises. "You're not alone, Suze, and you're not going to ever be alone again. I'm not leaving you. I'm never leaving you. Am I finally getting through?''

"Stix?" She had a hard time forming his name. The candle flickered wildly in the darkness, glinting on silver and shadows and the unbearably bright light in his eyes. He layered a series of kisses on the rim of her sweater at the throat. Eyes closed, she shivered, but not from chill. Their cave was no sauna, but the survival blanket reflected body heat—a lot of body heat. In fact, she'd never felt warmer. Her sweater had front buttons and he was busy finding them all. "Stix?" she repeated breathlessly.

"Yes?"

"You *know* this cave," she accused him.

"Slightly." He eased up to push off her boots, then his boots, and then he unfolded the second blanket. He knew she wasn't cold, but she would be. It wasn't necessary to remove all clothes to make love, but this was one time when total nakedness was absolutely necessary. When he draped the second blanket over both of them he started working on the zipper of her jeans.

She was busy kissing his neck, although her kisses were a little more annoyed than passionate. "How 'slightly' do you know this cave?"

"Hmm?" He discovered a pair of red satin underpants. They looked so good on that he was tempted to leave them. For about a second and a half.

"Answer me!"

Meekly he murmured, "If I were trussed and blindfolded, I could have you in fresh air in less than fifteen minutes. We took the complicated route in. There's a much easier way out."

"You let me think we were lost!"

"Yes."

"That wasn't very...ethical. Or very kind. Or very...principled."

"I know. And I'm trying very hard to give a hoot, Suze, but—"

"You expect me to trust you after this?"

"Yes."

"You expect me to love you after this?"

"Yes."

"I *do* love you."

"Sweetheart, I know that. I've known that for a long time. And I want you to tell me all about it in a minute or two, but for right now I'd just like you to show me." He whispered, "There's no buttons on this sweatshirt. It's going to be easier than you know."

There was an incorrigible grin on his mouth. Not for long. She wanted to laugh with him for the next hundred years, but not quite yet. Her mouth fused on his, urgently, wildly, luringly. Her first kiss had no patience. Neither did the second. She'd been too sure she'd lost him. She'd been too positive there would be no chance to love him again.

He pushed at his clothes, then she did. Neither were pleased until they were both bare, chest to chest, legs tangled in legs, heart against heart. He shuddered under the least caress of her fingertips, and her potent lover came alive—insatiably, passionately alive—for the first taste of her tongue.

"Don't you ever try to throw me out again, Susan," he whispered. "You're all I have. All I've ever had. I wouldn't know how to live without you."

She shushed him with touch and lips, matching urgency with hunger, heat with heat, need with want. It all blended. Their single candle made giant flickering shadows against the silver walls, shadows of a huge man, shadows of a small woman dancing in the dark to a rhythm as old as lovers. The cave had an inherent primal silence, ten thousand years of blackness and lonely stillness, broken now with the sounds of loving.

He called her name in the flame and shadowed darkness. He'd done that before, but she hadn't believed it. He'd also kissed her before like a man coming home, like a man being taken into the deep soft wells of emotion, but she hadn't believed that, either. He'd joined his body with hers before. She'd seen the intense harshness sculpt his features, the blaze of love in his eyes when he took her, but even that, before, she'd only wanted to believe.

The magic was real this time. She believed this time. The difference had to do with that stark, raw moment when she'd believed them both lost. The future was no looming dragon if he was with her. If it had come down to no tomorrow—if it had come down to last moments—she knew exactly where she wanted to be. Here. With him. Being held by him, where she could protect, hold, keep, cherish him.

Stix was a strong, vulnerable man who needed an incredible amount of love. No one could do that better than her. For a woman with a terribly battered ego, she'd suddenly never felt so strong and sure. No one could *possibly* love him more than she could. Her whole heart beat with the rhythm of exaltation, celebration, the hugeness of loving. She felt special. She felt beautiful. She felt loved. Stix hadn't given her the gift of confidence. No human being could do that for another. But loving took two, and the power of love she felt for Stix told her something about herself that she had desperately needed to know.

Their lips clung together. Their bodies stretched and slicked in ancient rhythms, the music of two. She'd never seen a man with such eyes. He looked at her as though she was his world. And she took him farther than he thought they could go, because the new Susan was a little more wild and wanton than the old. The new Susan intended to please, pleasure and make absolutely sure the man knew who he belonged to. There would be no straying. There would be no thinking of other women. Not in her bed. She was so sure of that that she had to show him.

Ecstasy came on a hiss and a hush of soaring toward sun. She called his name a thousand times and rode a streak of fire as real as he was. When it was done, he pulled the blanket over both of them and held her, their bodies hot, their hearts still heaving.

"I love you," she whispered fiercely.

He framed her face in his hands. "And I love you. Never doubt it, love."

It took long minutes for the slumberish, satiated weakness to pass. They shared smile after smile. She couldn't seem to stop looking at him. He didn't try.

Finally she found the strength to lift her hand, trace the line of her lower lip with her fingertip. "Are you going to marry me, shorty? Or are we just going to live in sin for the next ninety years?"

He nipped at her finger, his eyes as soft as silver. "That's a pretty aggressive question for a woman who was once too scared to believe in the future. Suddenly you don't seem so scared of tomorrow, Suze."

"No." She kissed him. Five, six times. Then another dozen.

"In fact, you don't seem particularly scared of anything. Or worried about anything. Or concerned about anything."

"No," she repeated.

He was doing his best to breathe between kisses, but his lungs were having a hard time remembering that fancy trick about inhaling and exhaling. "Did anything in particular bring out this wanton aggressive streak?" he asked delicately. "I've never known anyone who got things as confused as you do, honey. You're supposed to get excited over roses. Instead, you react to burned chicken and being tricked into a cave ninety feet underground."

"I don't have anything confused," she promised him. "I adored your roses, shorty. I adore you."

"You mean I'm not going to get any more lectures on phenylethylamine? No biological anthropological studies proving that love doesn't last? No threats about how happily ever afters don't exist in real life?"

"Stix," Susan said patiently, "do you have to have it said?"

"Please," he murmured. "And loudly."

"I believe in loving you. I believe in you and me. And I believe that a happily ever after will take care of itself, if we love each other enough, if we grow together, learn together, take care of each other. I know that's what I feel for you, what I want for you. I know that's what you want for me. To heck with the fairy tales—I know darn well we have something better. I *love* you. Now could we please stop talking?''

"I was hoping to get a repeat of that proposal—"

"*Later*, shorty."

* * * * *

FOUR UNIQUE SERIES
FOR EVERY WOMAN YOU ARE . . .

Silhouette Romance

Love, at its most tender, provocative,
emotional . . . in stories that will make you laugh and
cry while bringing you the magic of falling in love.

6 titles per month

Silhouette Special Edition

Sophisticated, substantial and packed with
emotion, these powerful novels of life and love will
capture your imagination and steal your heart.

6 titles per month

Silhouette Desire

Open the door to romance and passion. Humorous,
emotional, compelling—yet always a believable
and sensuous story—Silhouette Desire never
fails to deliver on the promise of love.

6 titles per month

Silhouette Intimate Moments

Enter a world of excitement, of romance
heightened by suspense, adventure and the
passions every woman dreams of. Let us
sweep you away.

4 titles per month

READERS' COMMENTS ON SILHOUETTE DESIRES

"Thank you for Silhouette Desires. They are the best thing that has happened to the bookshelves in a long time."
—V.W.*, Knoxville, TN

"Silhouette Desires—wonderful, fantastic—the best romance around."
—H.T.*, Margate, N.J.

"As a writer as well as a reader of romantic fiction, I found DESIREs most refreshingly realistic—and definitely as magical as the love captured on their pages."
—C.M.*, Silver Lake, N.Y.

"I just wanted to let you know how very much I enjoy your Silhouette Desire books. I read other romances, and I must say your books rate up at the top of the list."
—C.N.*, Anaheim, CA

"Desires are number one. I especially enjoy the endings because they just don't leave you with a kiss or embrace; they finish the story. Thank you for giving me such reading pleasure."
—M.S.*, Sandford, FL

*names available on request